Human Nat

Copyright © 2017 Lee Rimmington

This version of the text copyright © 2017 Lee Rimmington

The right of Lee Rimmington to be identified as the author of the work has been asserted by him in accordance with the Copyright, Design and Patents act of 1988

Apart from any use permitted under UK copyright law, this publication may only be reproduced, stored or transmitted, in any form, or by any means, with prior permission, or in the case of reprographic production, in accordance with the terms and licences issued by the Copyright Licence Agency

All characters in this publication are fictitious and any resemblance to real persons, living or dead, is purely coincidental

Dedicated to Lynne Langley, your constant faith in me more than makes up for my lack of talent

Chapter 1

Just one more day. Samuel was becoming so excited that he could not sit still, there were butterflies in his stomach and he found himself repeating the same task over and over again, he had not acted like this since he was a young boy on Christmas eve. The task in question was a basic one, he would empty a rucksack sort through all its contents and then place them all neatly inside.

After the thirty seventh time Samuel finally excepted that this was no way to spend his morning so he took off his clothes and slid into his hot spring, Samuel owned a hot spring. As he sat down on the stone steps the water's warmth filled his body he let out a loud sigh. He looked towards the sky, one of his favourite activities and saw thousands of tiny lights, anyone might assume that they were stars but this was impossible, firstly as it was early morning and secondly Samuel was not outside.

Samuel lived his life inside a cave, but this was not a harsh, barren hole where he struggled to eke out a living, no his cave was central heated, had its own renewable light source, the aforementioned pool with its collection of fish and a diving board, Yep Samuel had it made.

Back to the stars, they were actually glow worms that lived their entire lived on the ceiling, though this did confuse Samuel had he had never seen them pupate, they seemed to be locked in eternal childhood. The light they made was by no means great but it was enough to see and even read by.

Samuel scrubbed himself down with some homemade soap and then did a few laps. Around him pale fish moved causally out of the way as he passed, despite the fact that Samuel had been eating them for over three years they were still unafraid, Samuel paused in the middle of his swimming it never made him feel good to be eating things that trusted him so much but they were his only reliable source of protein and if it wasn't them it would just be some squirrel in the forest.

Before this he had never thought about where his food came from he had just gone to the supermarket but here there was no such convenience. Samuel had not been born here or anywhere near here, he did not know how it had happened but one day he had just shown up and thrown all the natives into disarray.

He slapped his hands on the water's surface and the fish darted away. Samuel returned to his swimming and completed his twenty laps before he rested again. The water around him steadied and, though a little distorted, he could make out his reflection in the water.

He was an altogether rather normal and unimpressive man, around five foot ten inches, mud brown hair that appeared to have been cut by an orangutan, brown eyes that might look good on a dead fish, a dull almost sickly face, not ugly by any sense of the word just uninteresting. His frame was evident of a very active lifestyle with strong legs, back and arms but his gut still had some flab on it and no matter how hard Samuel tried he could not get rid of it. On his left shoulder he could make out the faint impression of a scar caused by a shattered knife.

"Oh well that's enough ogling" Samuel said to himself and he climbed out the pool, the cave was arranged a bit like an old theatre, the pool was the cheap seats, the large flat area he stood on now was the stage and surrounding him on three side where a set of ledges, the one behind was always larger than the last. The way it was arranged and the sharp angles told Samuel that this was not natural formation it was man made, Samuel supposed it had been some sort of leisure retreat or the like, it certainly would have taken a lot of time and money to build.

Samuel began to climb the ledges, heading in the direction of the diving board. Samuel had to be carefully, the steam from the spring made the rock slippery and if he fell he would almost certainly crack his head open but he had done this many times before and had become sure footed as a result.

He reached the diving board and was now several metre of the ground. He looked directly in front of himself and could see a large opening in the wall, that in turn led to the outside world. Walking to the boards edge he looked down, a faint sense of vertigo overcame him but he suppressed it. The board was made of rock so it obviously provided little lift as he leapt of the rock, did several summersaults and dived into the water.

As he plunged through the water he felt the heat rise and directly in front of him he saw a deep fissure in the rock and out from it he could see hazy water flowing from it, he adjusted himself and the momentum carried back towards the surface.

Taking in a deep breath of air Samuel swam back to the steps and climbed out of the water. He walked towards the cave exit, he wet feet slapped against the floor and the sound echoed throughout the cavern. But he did not pass through it, not yet, he stopped by the nearest ledge. Arranged on it were several items including clothes, towels, and a set of body armour. For now, Samuel took a towel from the pile and walked down the corridor.

The light from the worms only stretched a few metres up the corridor beyond which there was total darkness but that did not worry Samuel, without a moment's hesitation he stepped into the inky blackness. Once he had taken around ten steps the air changed, the moisture was stripped away. With the total lack of humidity Samuel felt the water being stripped from the surface of his skin. His eyes began to dry out and he had to blink rapidly, his lips and mouth became dry as well and he desperately wanted a drink.

Samuel began to rub himself down and within a minute he was bone dry. He dashed back the way he came and leaving the towel on the floor he took a big gulp of water from the pool. It was not bad warm but much better cold.

Picking up his towel and folding it neatly he placed it back on the pile. Samuel got dressed almost all of his clothes were handmade, the only exceptions were a red polo shirt, a black hoodie, a pair trouser and some trainers, which were only worn for special occasions. He ignored these clothes and instead but on the ultramarine tunic and black trousers he had worn earlier. He also slipped on some very simple socks, his old machine made ones had been worn day after day, he had washed them of course, for over two years and they had finally worn out. Not bad for a pair of cheap socks.

But he had no time to mill about here, admiring his fish, no Samuel had more preparations to make before his trip. Samuel put on a pair of excellently crafted leather boot, this too had been made by Samuel and he had spent years perfecting the technique, these could handle just about anything and they were comfortable too.

He attached a belt around his waist, a thick and well-worn piece of leather that a served him well for several years. There was also a knife attached to the belt, a gift from a friend, a pouch that stored his fire lighting supplies and a custom-made hook for a water canteen he took almost everywhere. Picking up the bottle he filled it with water from the pool and headed down the corridor.

The corridor was also called the dry room, for obvious reasons, and while it was and would always be a pain to walk down it was far better that spending his winters up top. He usually had a bad time with winter, his friend Tamara was unable to travel through the snow to meet him and the loneliness wreaked havoc with his mind. However, the last one had been different, Samuel had made a new friend, Vana, and she was able to bulldoze her was through the cold. It felt good to have friends like that.

A short distance down Samuel leapt into the air and then landed a few feet further down, Samuel had done so because he kept his mattress here in order to prevent it from become damp and infested with mildew. At least that was the theory because he kept his clothes in the cavern and they were just fine, so Samuel supposed it was more out of habit nowadays.

His footsteps echoed around him and to pass the time he shouted down the corridor, waiting for his voice to shout back at him, it made him chuckle.

Up ahead Samuel made out a faint beam of light, he had reached the end of the dry room. Even though the light was faint and he could see very little he knew that there was a set of steps in front of him. Placing his hands above his head his palms came into contact with a smooth, flat stone. He took a few steps up and pushed, the stone lifted a gust of cool wind washed over his face and Samuel slid the slab behind him, there was a loud scrapping sound. Samuel kept his eyes closed as the sudden change in light would stun him otherwise.

Stepping into the sunlight, Samuel gradually opened his eyes to reveal a scene of breath-taking beauty. A forest, like those described in fairy tales, the trees were lush and green, thick carpets of grass stretched as far as the eye could see and surrounding the sturdy trunks was a halo of flowers, each one gorgeous and in full bloom.

It was wrong, it was miraculous, but it was wrong, it looked as though it had been made by man rather than grown by nature and Samuel was certain that this was exactly the case. Who? or Why? These were questions he did not know the answer too but he was confident that he would someday.

Samuel stood inside a cave, fairly large with many objects scattered throughout, including a wood store at the back, far away from the rain, several buckets and chests containing various items, several tools such as shovels, rakes and hoes. The cave, unlike the cavern and forest, was a natural formation, he could tell by its rough edges and the eroded rock.

Sitting in front of the cave mouth was a fire pit, a simple construct that provided him with both warmth, light and a means to cook his food. There were several charred logs in the pit and above was a spit with several hooks to hold pots.

To either side were a pair of post and hanging between them was a rolled-up piece of tarpaulin, or rather the closet thing he could get, on rainy day he would attach it to two other post and it would keep the rain off his fire but also stop it from pouring directly into the cave, when it rained here it came down hard.

Samuel sat down on a rock, that served as a chair, directly in front of the pit. He considered lighting the fire but felt there was not point, it was the middle of summer and even with the cooling breeze was struggling to keep his temperature down.

It was midday and he needed to do something to keep him busy. Samuel got back up and began to make certain that everything was in order, Samuel would be leaving tomorrow and he would not be returning for several weeks so he had to take stock and make certain he had everything he needed.

After much talking, Samuel had been able to convince Vana and Tamara to accompany him on an expedition around the shore of a massive lake a few miles away. Tamara was relatively easy to convince but Vana had been far more cautious and had spent several days stating all the things that could go wrong, she turned out to be surprisingly imaginative in this field. However, in the end she agreed when she realised that the two of them were going regardless and felt that at least she could look after them when they went.

He straightened out the cave and swept out the dust, this was a task he did everyday as dirt seemed to love setting up shop in his home. When he got back he figured there would be a mountain of the stuff "oh well" he said to himself, he quite liked sweeping up, there was something cathartic about doing a simple repetitive task.

The broom was placed back in its rightful spot but then Samuel realised that without him to check on it every day it might be best to keep all of his things out of sight, not because they would be stolen but because the weather could get rough and they might be damaged, so he started the long task of bringing all of his tools into the dry room. It was a quick but tiring job but he managed to move everything he wanted downstairs, he left the log pile, as it was not likely to be damaged, it did not really matter it if was and he could easily get more.

Samuel believed he had earned himself a snack so he dusted off his hands and walking into the forest. Under the leaves, the breeze was cut off and he found the air became stagnant, the pollen from the flowers thickened the air with the scent of Lavender, honeysuckle, and a dozen other smells his nose could not pick out. Above him he could hear the warning calls of birds and the rustling of the trees told him the squirrels were getting out of the way.

It was not just the beauty of the forest that was wrong, it was how it grew, the trees were arranged symmetrically each one four and a half long steps from its neighbours. Samuel wiped the sweat that was starting to pour from brow and he took a sip from his canteen.

As he hooked the canteen back to his belt he noticed some black lumps in the corner of his eye. He turned and exclaimed "oh sweet!" he dived down and began to collect some brown, rather ugly, mushrooms. They were called "horn of plenty" and they were some of the best food in this forest. Even better there were lots of them, more than he had ever found in a single space before.

Samuel stuffed his pockets but also left enough that there would still be some when he came back, he would treat himself tonight but he would also save some for tomorrow and surprise Vana. Tamara however was not fond of mushrooms so he did not need to worry about her.

While that had added a much-needed boost to his dinner it was not what he had set out for so he continued deeper into the forest. After several minutes, he found what he was looking for, an orange tree, its branched filled with bright orange fruit far larger anything in his home world.

"World" Samuel said that word aloud, normally when someone said that you thought of aliens but that could not be the case he had seen many familiar animals and the biggest clue was that the exact same moon hung in the sky along with the few constellations he could recognise.

His growling stomach made him focus on the tree, he could not reach any of the fruit from the ground but this was not a problem. Samuel took a few steps back and the ran at the tree, his foot hit the trunk and he then used that a way to catapult himself higher. He grabbed onto a branch and the hauled himself up. He stood up on the bough and began to search on a particularly good specimen.

He discovered several fine examples but he could afford to be picky so he climbed higher looking for something better. Samuel, found it tantalising out of reach yet he had faced this problem before. He took out his knife, Samuel could feel the engraving Tamara had personally carved into the handle, a very crude image of Samuel and he treasured it immeasurably.

With one swift movement, he cut the orange from the branch and with impressive reflexes he caught it. "Oh yeah, that's how it's done" Samuel said smugly towards the sky. He clambered down once Samuel was a few metres from the ground his brain finally twigged that it was above the ground and the same sense of vertigo overcame him, he may have conquered his fear but that did not mean it had left.

Samuel jump and fell towards ground, he had done this hundreds of times but on this occasion he made a slight mistake with his legs. He feet hit the grass, sending shockwaves up his body, and tumbled backward. It hurt but he could tell that it was just a temporary injury "well that's what I get for being smug" he told himself.

Once the pain had died down he sat underneath the orange tree and ate his prize. The rind came away extremely easily but he did not throw it away, he would keep it and later on, not tonight, he would add a few shaving to some fish, it really perked it up. Samuel took one of the enormous wedges from the rest of the fruit and though it took a bit of stretching put it all in his mouth.

Heavenly, that was the best way he could describe it, the fruit had the perfect mixture of sweetness and tartness, neither one completely overpowered the other. It was strange Samuel knew it would taste fantastic, by all rights he should be used to it by now but it, somehow, always managed to be a fun experience, eating the food here was truly a joy.

Samuel took it easy for a while, just sitting taking in the view, when he was not moving Samuel found the forest quite pleasant. He watched a greater spotted woodpecker drilling a hole in the side of an Aspen tree. "Remarkable birds" Samuel said, he had done a paper about them for his master's degree at university though more for pleasure than a requirement. Their heads moved so quickly they experienced and could withstand one thousand two hundred G, humans pass out and die at nine and because of this they could not get concussions.

It seemed just like yesterday he was attending his lectures, spending late nights to get his assignment done on time, though this was because he wrote ten times more than anyone else. Samuel adored biology, he had done ever since he had first learned about the subject in primary school.

Since that day he spent almost every free moments learning all he could about the subject, he watched every documentary on television, read every book his local library had, three times over and had even done his own research in his back garden, when he was eleven he had performed a population survey on reptiles and amphibians for a year and sent the data to a local research board. Two months later he a received a certificate making him an honorary member and was told that when he grew up he could put it on his CV and was then offered for a tour of their facility, though run down sheep shed was probably a more accurate way to describe it.

Samuel had kept his passion up even here, where everything else about his life had been stripped away that was the one thing he clung madly too. He had an entire book filled with information about the biology and lifestyle habits of the people who lived here. Tamara also had several other books that Samuel had written they contained information about the plants animals and fungi.

This was in fact the reason Samuel had arranged the trip he would explore the lake cataloguing all of the living this he found, he could hardly wait.

"Life was so simple back then" Samuel said with a smile. He gentle slapped his cheeks "oh well no use living in the past" he added picking himself up. Samuel headed back home. He left the forest and noticed for the first time in a few months the mountain that covered his home, it was amazing how you could become so blind to things you saw every day. Like the cave this too was a natural formation, it had clearly been here for thousands, possibly millions, of years and was most likely the remains of a once great mountain range. The locals called it the old mountain and they believed that it was formed for the body of some ancient giant, whether it was supposed to be dead or just sleeping he was not sure.

Once he reached the cave he dumped the mushrooms into one of the boxes he had moved into the dry room and left the cave, on his left was a garden in which he grew all of his crops, it had expanded over the years to include more vegetables, he even had a small patch of mint.

Surrounding the garden was a wicker fence, that kept the deer and other large animals out.

He opened a simple gate that allowed him entry and began to inspect the plant, looking after them took a lot of diligence. This was his only concern when he left, without his care he was certain he would lose most of his crop but this was not a problem the summer was so long and the plants grew so fast that he could have four harvest in a year.

Despite only inspecting it this morning he found that several slugs had managed to squeeze their way in. He removed them and placed them one the forest edge, he then went back into the cave, collected a bucket filled with ash and put a thick ring around his garden, this would help deter any more that tried to get a quick meal.

Samuel refilled the bucket with ash from the fire pit and put it back. He was happy his plants were doing well, he would bring some of them when he departed. Funny thing was that survival, if you knew what you were doing, did not take up much time in truth most of his day was free time he could spend on anything he wanted. Problem was there was very little to do.

"Maybe I could do a little research on my entomological study" Samuel said to the sky but he waved aside this notion doing a local study would take more than a few hours, by the time he got back he would have forgotten most of it and he would be doing that anyway when he left.

Perhaps he could invent something new, well reinvent, it was not a bad idea but unfortunately he had been drawing up blanks for several weeks, Samuel was not a natural engineer, though to his credit he had done well in that field. He shrugged his shoulders, there was only one thing to do when he had absolutely nothing else, carving.

He selected a piece of wood from his pile took out his knife and began to carve. With this amount of wood, he could make three small figurines, he remembered the woodpecker from earlier and felt that was a good idea. Samuel had become extremely skilled and could make things as fine a specialist fish hooks from animal bone, when he tired of the fish form the pool or the guilt got to him, he would take a sinew fishing line and one of his hooks and see what he could catch.

In under an hour Samuel had finished, this was not some crude design, he had included details for feathers, the scales on its feet, and if it was not brown you could have confused it for a real woodpecker. With one final cut the sculpture came away, he placed it on one of the rocks and smiled.

As he began to carve a swallow he suddenly shouted "oh bugger I forgot." Samuel almost threw the wood to the floor, placed his knife back on his belt and ran into the forest. He was taking a different direction to the orange tree, it was farther afield and Samuel was just glad he still had his canteen with him.

What had torn him away from his quiet time was not some vital life or death item it was simply a promise he had made to himself, fairly trivial if he thought about it and Samuel was happy no one had been around to see how he had reacted.

Samuel smelled it before he saw it. A mixture of rotting meat and vomit, however rather than drive him away the smell drew him closer. Out of place between the oaks and aspens was a durian plant. There were several huge, green, spiked fruit. Though the smell would make you think that a rat a died in them, it actually meant they were ripe.

A year ago Samuel had planted a durian tree closer to home but it had not yet reached maturity. Collecting a particularly large durian Samuel quickly scarpered and put as much distance between him and the smell. He cracked open the fruit and a fresh wave of rotten mulch pieced his nose, he sneezed and the began to eat the large yellow, grub like fruit inside.

This was his favourite food, it tasted like caramel and was the closest he could get to chocolate. "Oh, how I miss chocolate" Samuel moaned. Inside each lump of pulp was a large brown seed, it was inedible and Samuel had no need of it so he threw it away.

When he left the forest, the sun was starting to sink, it would still be several hours before bedtime and he would soon have to think about tea, though he would probably eat less of it now, he had intended to have the durian for dinner. Oh well that just meant more mushrooms tomorrow, Vana would be happy.

After Samuel arrived home he took some tinder from his pouch along with a piece of flint and a metal striker, an item shaped a little like a horseshoe. He struck the flint with his striker and a few sparks flew from the metal. As the tinder steadily burned he add more and more wood until a healthy fire crackled in front of him.

He picked up a metal stand and hung it over the fire, Samuel then put a fry pan on top of it, filled with a little beef fat, then sliced a few mushrooms and threw them into the pan. Inspecting the blade with his thumb he found it was a little dull, from one of his pockets he took out a portable wet stone and sharpened his blade.

While he took great care to get a razor-sharp edge, he never forgot to stir his food. When the time the mushrooms where finished he did not stop sharpening his knife he just removed the pan from the heat and every once in a while, he would pop one in his mouth.

Samuel plucked out one of his hairs and the gently brushed the knife edge against it, the hair split in two and he watched it gracefully fall to the ground "oh yeah" Samuel said. He methodically and thoroughly cleaned his cooking utensils, he used to have a machine for this.

With that finished he spent his last moments of sunlight carving, he finished the swallow figure, not too bad if he said so himself.

The sun was still up but Samuel was beginning to feel tired so he decided to call it an early night, the fire was already dying so he just left it to burn out by itself. Samuel slid the slab back in place and walked down the dry room.

He entered the cavern, the moist air was a welcome relief, but he was carrying a satchel, something he had not had when he entered it. This was where he kept his book and writing supplied, so that they did not get damaged in the moist air. Samuel had to reinvented the quill, paper and ink pot as the villagers did not use writing, not because they were stupid it was just their memories were so good they had no real use for it. He on the other hand lacked that ability so it had become a necessity if he wanted to continue his research.

Sitting down on one of the ledges he opened the bag and took out a large, leather bound book. On the cover, it read "An Anthropological Encyclopaedia of Sapient Races." Samuel thought that he may have misspelled

Encyclopaedia he did not think so but there was not a lot he could do about it; he did not have a dictionary after all.

Anyway, this was not what he was after, instead he began to count the sheets of paper he had and supplies of ink. Making paper was a time-consuming process but he had managed to make over forty sheets and he had over five pots of ink, that should be enough he would only be doing rough data gathering, he could organise it all when he got back. Even if it did not Tamara would be bringing her own supply.

It all seemed to be in order so he placed all the paper back into the satchel, except for one sheet that had writing on it. It was a check list to make sure he had everything he needed before he left.

He collected the huge rucksack he had been so obsessively been repacking earlier and removed all the contents "Ok let's do the this properly" said Samuel.

"Two changes of clothes, check" Samuel placed a tick by the side. "Various medical supplies, check." "Ten metres of rope, check." "Writing Supplies, check." "Armour" he left blank for now he would check that off when he actually left. "Thin mattress, check." "Twenty metres of fishing line with assorted hooks, check." "Blanket, towel and soap, check." "Food supplies, will deal with tomorrow." "Walking stick same as before." "Cutting tools including knife, machete, wire saw and wet stone, check." "Fire starting equipment, check." There were a few other but these were the most important.

It was a tight fit getting everything to fit inside but fortunately he had played plenty of Tetris in his youth and he managed to leave just enough room for the food. It was heavy, very heavy and Samuel knew that it would put him through his paces however he had been practicing hauling it around so he was fairly confident that he could manage.

Resting the rucksack against the wall, Samuel removed his boots and socks, wriggled his toes savouring the freedom. He removed his clothes, folded the up neatly and then put of a pair of pyjamas, "that feels better" said Samuel as he felt the heat radiate off.

The gentle blue light was far better than any sleeping pill, Samuel yawned and stretched. He gathered his mattress from the corridor and while he was at it put his writing supplied back, laid it out by one of the ledges. He made sure one of his cups was filled with water and settled down for sleep.

Unfortunately, Samuel found this to be very difficult, despite how tired he felt and how heavy his eyelids were. He tossed and turned, tried several different sleeping positions but his nerves would not let him. He raised his right and looked at his crooked ring finger and rubbed it, when he was younger Samuel had broken it in an accident, now whenever he was stressed he rubbed it and it provided him with comfort. He sighed and said "this is going to be a rough night."

Chapter 2

Just one more day. Vana sat in her kitchen finishing off the rest of her breakfast she smiled at the greatness of it all, not the food itself, it was just a loaf of bread and a few fresh fruits, but rather the circumstances that had led to it.

This time last year she had been scrounging around in the wilderness barely managing to survive being chased from one area to another but now she lived in a house larger than any she had ever dreamed of; she had not felt true hunger in over a year and her dreams were peaceful and sweet. For all this she had two people to thank.

Tamara a young girl the age of thirteen, daughter of one of the village heads, Pancha, was the first without her the adjustment to village life would have been far more difficult and the rest of the villagers would not have given her a chance. Not because she had committed a great crime but because of what she was, Vana was Dingonek.

Vana had flame red hair that came just passed her shoulders, tied into a plait at the back. Her eyes were the same colour and seemed to flick and glow like a true fire but she had slit pupils like a cat. Her arms, form her fingertips to her elbows, were covered in a substance called chitin, the same shade of red as her hair, and looked like gauntlets worn by a knight. Near her wrists were two opening and from them came a single claw that she could use either as a tool or a weapon.

Her legs were also covered in chitin from her knees downwards, with her toes ending in claws, they were sharp but she used them more for climbing and keeping her footing than anything else. Finally, to top all of that off, at the base of her back came a large tail, strikingly similar to a scorpion, with a huge stinger on the end capable of delivering an extremely powerful venom.

However, it was not her appearance that had caused everyone to distrust her, in that regard she was fairly average actually, it was the reputation her people had as aggressive thieves and liars, a lie but Vana had found people were hard to sway in their beliefs.

Yet the one person she would be forever grateful to was Samuel, while Tamara had been a huge help and Vana would not have gotten this far without her, it had been Samuel who had believed in her, that ignored the rumours and reached out to her, he had been the first person she had ever met that treated her like a person. Vana chuckled the thought of the literal embodiment of evil being the most compassionate thing in the world always made her smile.

Samuel was a human and as every child new humans were the most horrific monsters ever spawned, they only existed to destroy and corrupt and as Vana discovered every child was wrong.

Vana finished off her breakfast and the kettle finished boiling "convenient" Vana said. She picked up her dishes and washed them in the sink. The morning light shone the window, faint specks of dust were visible in the beams and outside she could hear the village slowly coming to life. In under an hour the market place would be filled with people looking for items they needed from the stalls there. Vana had initially found the whole experience daunting, over one hundred people all trying to talk over one another had frightened her in a way she had never experienced before but over time she had gotten used to it and even started to enjoy it.

As she dried the dish her mind turned to tomorrow and the trip she would soon take, it was funny she had spent her entire life living in the wild, huddled under trees and she had hoped that she would never do so again. Yet when she thought about traveling with her friends for some reason it made her excited, strange what good company could do.

She had prepared just as much as Samuel and there as a large backpack in her living room filled with everything she would need but unlike Samuel she did not check it and she had no list, she did not need to her memory was flawless and she knew she had forgotten nothing.

The plate was placed back in the cupboard, she pushed open a door that lead to her back garden, it was by no means huge but a pair of children could certainly chase each other around it. Her home was made out of wood, two storeys tall with windows for every room, there was no glass, Vana did not know what glass was, so in order to keep the rain out there was shutters over each window.

Beneath her wall was a long patch of flowers, gardening was a very common pass time in the village and Vana was no exception. She had been clueless at first, she only knew flowers by whether they were edible and if they tasted good. Vana had a wide selection, from tulips to orchids but they were not all ornamental she also had basil, thyme, cumin and chicory just to add some flavour to her meals.

She took a small copper watering can and gave all the plants a much-needed drink, in the height of summer the soil dried out incredibly quickly.

"Good morning Vana" a voice called from over the fence. Vana looked up from her posies to see her neighbours Eoin and Takiyak. They were a young couple around twenty-five years old but they were not the same as Vana, she was the only Dingonek here, they were Boreray, they had several traits of sheep.

On Eoin's head were a pair of curled horns, they were a slight shade of red, his head was filled with curly white hair. His eyes were yellow with horizontal pupils identical to a sheep. He wore no tunic, his chest was covered with the same hair as his head so a tunic was unnecessary, and in summer down right uncomfortable, instead he wore a black skirt that came to his knees. His legs were unlike a humans', they appeared to have two knees and he had hooves instead of feet. Takiyak looked similar except she had black horns, blue eyes and wore a blue skirt.

Like most people Takiyak and Eoin had initially been distrustful of Vana but having to live next to her had forced them to get know her, the desire to be a good neighbour overrode their caution.

"Hello" Vana replied with a smile "what are you too doing up so early" she asked, it was common for them to spend their mornings in bed, Vana could guess what they were up to. "Well we have to get some of that fertiliser for our flowers" Takiyak answered. "If we don't get their early they will be all out" Eoin added finishing his wife sentence.

Vana stared at them and said "I can't tell whether that was adorable or creepy." The pair chuckled and Eoin replied "well we have no idea how you knew what was wrong with our crops, some of us whispered that you had dark knowledge" he waved his fingers in an unsuccessful attempt to be scary.

Suddenly Vana felt very depressed, Eoin had unintentionally upset her. Not the dark knowledge but that he and everyone else believed that she had solved the crop problem. A year ago, just about a week after Vana had met Samuel and Tamara, they had learned that the crops were failing and Samuel had correctly deduced that the ground was becoming barren.

Yet when the time came to reveal the solution Samuel had decided that it was best for Vana take the credit so that Vana could prove she was a good person and have a place in the village. While this was a lovely gesture and showed how kind Samuel was she hated taking the credit for something she did not do and though Samuel constantly reassured her that it was fine and she did help, it provided little comfort.

"Are you alright dear?" Takiyak asked. This was an example of another of these people's remarkable abilities, though Vana facial expressions and body language had been subtle, so subtle that a human could not have detect them, to Eoin and Takiyak it was a visible as a lighthouse on a clear night. "I'm sorry I didn't mean to offend you" said Eoin.

Vana smiles and told them "no that's not it, just... thinking about something else." She rubbed her forehead and added "are you sure you don't mind looking after my flowers" she added changing the subject. "Oh yeah don't worry about it" Takiyak replied. "You can help yourself to any herbs" she paused for a moment "so long as you don't take all of it." "Thanks" Takiyak said.

They spent a few more minutes chatting before the pair of them had to leave, Vana waved them goodbye and was left alone again. She finished watering her plants and then went back inside and sat back down at the table.

There was nothing to do until Tamara woke up and came to visit. Tamara was a Lamia, she was part snake and just like a snake she had to wait for the sun to warm her up before she could do anything. While Vana could easily live of the gratitude she had received for saving the village and occasionally going to Samuel when a new invention was required to keep up her image of the problem solver, instead she spent her days assisting Tamara, it made her feel valuable.

Yes, though Samuel's memory was not great his imagination was on a whole other level, the things his mind came up with, Vana believed it must be exhausting. The only other person who came close to Samuel's creativity was Tamara "maybe that's why she was the first person to see him for what he was" Vana mused.

She rapped on her table and made noises, "guess I'll straighten out the house" Vana said as she slammed her hands on the table. She picked up a broom the stood beside a wall and began to sweep. Though she had five large rooms it did not take her long to clean them, she finished the kitchen, living room, her bedroom and the two guest bedrooms in under half an hour "I need more stuff" she mumbled as he wiped down a shelf that held her few pointless trinkets.

Most were wooden carvings given to her by Samuel she also had a few shiny stones that Tamara had found for her, "maybe I should start collecting something as well" Vana said as she put a wooden rabbit back.

"You can forget about it" Vana said and from behind her she heard a voice say "how do you people do that?" she turned around so see a young Lamia standing behind her. She had golden hair, that seemed to glisten in the light, it had been intricately braided to that two strands of hair seemed to hang from the sides her head and she also had a much larger one at the back that reached her shoulder blades.

Her eyes were similar to Vana's only they were also a bright gold, the black pupil provided an astonishing contrast. She was fairly unremarkable from her head to her waist, though she was wearing a purple tunic with a black diamond in the middle. However, below her waist thing became interesting, in place of legs she had a large tail, identical to a snake, she had golden scales along her back with almost white ones on her stomach.

Tamara was certainly growing up fast, though for a Lamia height was more a matter of choice than genetics. As usual Tamara stood just slightly lower than Vana, she did this so people would still think of her as little girl and treat her better, though it had no effect on her mother.

In response to her question Vana replied "because you are predictable" giving a cheeky smile. "We'll see about that" Tamara retorted. Vana put the cloth she was using down on a table and then asked Tamara "what have you got for us today?" Tamara ran her fingers through her hair and replied "not a lot, just the usual walk around the place looking for problems to fix." Vana smiles and said "is it ever any different?" Tamara smiled back and said "only when Samuel's involved."

Outside of her house Vana found another person waiting, it was Pancha, Tamara's mother, she was almost identical to Tamara only she was larger, her hair was longer and kept loose and she was wearing and aquamarine tunic, though it still had the same diamond pattern on the front, it was a symbol of the Lamias and the family of the village heads always wore it.

"You know you didn't have to wait outside" Vana said as she shut her door. "Well it just didn't seem necessary" Pancha said "besides it's such a nice day out." "Well come on then, we can't stand here yakking" Tamara said pushing Vana and Pancha forward.

Even though the market was some distance away they could still here the hustle and as the drew closer it got louder, until they had to raise their voices to be heard. The market was a hive of activity, over one hundred people hurrying about looking for the thing they would need for another day.

Everyone stopped to say hello to the trio, politeness was a big thing in this village. Before they actually got to the business of helping people the three of them spent the first hour or so seeing to their own needs. Tamara and Pancha had nothing they needed today, so they just followed Vana as she headed towards a stall. Sitting down on an attractive mat was a young Cicindeli man.

He had artichoke green hair, from his head came two antennae, that moved gently scanning his environment. His eyes were totally different from anyone else's, they were compounded like a beetle, the light that reflected off them made them appear to possess every colour of the rainbow. His arms were similar to Vana's though they lacked the groove where he claws came out and were the same colour as his hair. He also had almost identical legs expect he had two large toes in place of Vana's five with a third one on his heel.

"Hello Lochlan" Vana said with a smile. Lochlan was still setting up, removing clay jars from a wooden crate, so he was little startled, usually no one bothered him until he was ready. "Oh good morning Vana what can I do for you today?" Lochlan said. "Could I get some blackberry jam please?" Vana asked. "Certainly" he replied and fished through a box to produce a what she wanted "there you are and how are you this fine morning?"

"I'm doing alright, just making sure me and Tamara have everything in place" said Vana. Lochlan's antennae began to twitch franticly and he scratched his chin "Oh yes the whole trip thing, I just don't see the point of it myself" he said waving his right hand. "It's simple really because if anything like the food shortage happens again we will already know about what is out there and we can plan accordingly" Vana said giving the official reason for the expedition.

Shaking his head and smiling Lochlan said "it doesn't matter because if something as bad as that happens you will just think up a solution." Vana looked at the ground and said "I wonder about that" she paused for a moment and then added "anyway I must get going I hope you have a pleasant day."

No money changed hands, the villager did not understand the concept, there was also no bartering, the farmers, foragers and craftsmen gave their items away. The idea being that at some point they could call in the favour. For example, one person would give a carpenter all the food they would need and in return the carpenter would make anything they needed.

"You know you really should take more credit for what happened" Tamara told Vana as she returned. "I know you have told me that a thousand times but I wasn't my idea" Vana hushed her voice and added "it was Samuel's." "You are absolutely right" Tamara said with a nod "but who was the one who actually got it to work?" she asked. "I don't really see…" Vana said but Tamara cut her off "who was it?" Vana slumped her shoulders and said "me… but." "No buts" Tamara said and she pushed Vana along.

Pancha then added "besides you have helped around here, remember when that bull ox escaped and you wrestled it to the ground, it could have caused some serious damage if you hadn't stopped it." She could not argue with that, the one thing Vana had that she owed to no one was her strength, Vana was by far the strongest person around able to lift a cow above her head with ease. Vana felt a little better and started to smile again "there we go" Tamara said.

Just then a Lamia woman came up to them she was middle aged with white hair and scales. This was a common occurrence, as the leader of the Lamias Pancha's job was to sort out any problems that occurred, of course if a Boreray or Cicindeli required assistance she would not ignore them. However, this did not happen often as the villagers knew that she had a hard-enough time dealing with the Lamia's problems, so usually they just kept looking until they found their own representative.

"How are you Mackenna?" Pancha asked calmly, knowing that she was rarely bothered with good news. "Not well Pancha, I've got moles in my garden, they're tearing up my grass and I need to get rid of them" Mackenna explained. "You too, I have over twenty complaints about moles this in the past five days" Pancha said. "Yes I heard about that" said Mackenna.

"Well you can always poison them" Pancha suggested. Mackenna appeared surprised and distressed by this and she shook her head and said "oh no I don't want to kill them, they can be helpful, eating pests… besides I think they're cute." "If that's the case then you could get some castor oil mix it with water and the sprinkle it on your grass that might drive them away, that what my mom does" Pancha said. "Ok I'll try that" Mackenna said with a grin and left.

When everything was going well that was a bad as the problems got around here, though Tamara had to admit the number of terrible things had increased dramatically since Samuel showed up.

They reached the end of the street and ahead was the forest, between that and them was a dirt path. From the right came an ox pulling a cart filled with "animal leavings." It may not have seemed like anything special but until a year ago carts and work animals were unheard of. When the crop crisis had occurred, Samuel had not only deduced that the soil was losing nutrients but that in order to shift enough fertiliser in time they would need a something new and that turned out to be a cart.

Vana had taken credit for this as well, though Tamara had received some of the praise as she helped build it. On top of that Vana also told them about work animals and crop rotation, which as any farmer will tell you is vital, until that they had just planted the same crops in the same field year after year. Since then the village had over twelve carts for various purposes with another six well on the way. Over time Samuel recommended improvements to his basic design, it had suspension and the wheels were now covered in a sort of metal tire, that protected the wood. All in all, Samuel had become quite the engineer.

They said hello to the Boreray woman guiding the animal pulling it and watched them disappear from sight and they were not the only ones; carts were still a novelty. "Still getting used to that" a voice called from behind them. Tamara turned first, as the statement seemed to have been addressed to her, to see a Cicindeli boy, fifteen years of age with crimson hair and chitin, he wore a blue tunic and on the front, were five circle stacked on top of one another. "Hello Tide you look good today" Tamara said with a smile.

Behind Tide came a Cicindeli man, Handus, Tide's father and another village head, Tide got his hair and Chitin colour from him. "You're all looking energetic this morning" Handus said as he drew closer. "Really?" Pancha said. "No I just couldn't think of anything meaningful to say" Handus replied.

"You two all set for tomorrow?" Tide asked Tamara and Vana. "Yeah we're all packed just trying to deal with the nerves" Tamara answered "why do want to come with us?" she added. Tide looked at the clouds, thought about it for a bit and replied "a little but I personally I like to know when my next meal will be." "So do I but that's what makes it an adventure" Vana said rolling her eyes. "I realise that but being gone thirty days" Tide said "what if you are fifteen days in and you are still less than half way there?" A good question, one that nobody else had asked yet however Tamara had prepared an answer "we just turn back." "Excellent strategy" said Handus.

"I am looking forward to seeing that map you'll be making" Tide said. They had several goals will the expedition, first to document all the life they found, second to map out the geography and third to mark out any spots that could serve as future village sights in case anything unforeseen occurred.

Tamara already had one in her room, a piece of parchment made from the complete skin of cow, that showed the village and the surrounding land with surprising detail, though Samuel had said that any real cartographer would have laughed at it. They would not be bringing that with them it was far too large, instead they would use paper to make rough sections and then add it when they got back.

Then a Cicindeli man interrupted them and asked Handus and Tide for help with a problem he was having, he said it was private, an unusual statement one that would almost certainly generate a lot of gossip by the people in earshot, about "the mysterious request", in the following week. They said goodbye and went somewhere they could be alone.

Immediately after another Lamia turned up with another problem which Pancha and Tamara quickly solved, they had a lot of experience. The rest of the morning was spent dealing with other complications, which fortunately were minor.

By afternoon Tamar and Vana left Pancha, at this point anyone who needed help had already asked for it so as Pancha went to visit her friends Tamara did the same. She asked if Vana would like to come with her and she happily accepted.

Unfortunately, the days when Tamara could spend the entire afternoon just playing with her friends were coming to an end, they were all getting older and now they had to start working. There was however a way around it, while Tamara could not drag them away from their jobs she could go and visit them and distract them for a bit.

The closest one was Becanda who conveniently enough lived right next door to Tamara. They arrived at her house but instead of knocking on the door she walked into the back garden to find Becanda and Mrs Caltha, a few tools in hand, making furniture from wood.

Becanda was an eleven years' old she had the stereotypical short woolly hair with yellow horn on her head, tied into her hair were several colourful ribbons, she wore a leather apron to protect her clothes and wool from sap and sawdust. Caltha was extraordinarily similar too her daughter much in the same way the Pancha looked like Tamara. She too wore an apron but this one was far older, with cracks running along its length.

The two of them were so busy that they did not notice Tamara or Vana standing in the middle of their back garden. Their set up was far simpler than that of the best carpenter in the village, Mr Faisal, but they still had a reputation for doing good work.

Tamara had and urge to make Becanda jump but she realised how stupid this was as she was hold some dangerous tools so instead she just walked up behind her and tapped Becanda's shoulder.

"You finished those dovetail joints mom?" Becanda asked without looking up from her work. "Not yet but I'm working on it" Tamara replied. Becanda looked up, her mom sounded a lot younger than she remembered, she turned around to find not her mom but Tamara was standing behind her instead.

It took her a few moments to process this but when she did she dropped her tools and gave her a tight hug. Caltha, hearing the commotion feared that her daughter had been in an accident but she took one look and then went straight back to work. "You only saw me yesterday" Tamara said hugging her back and giggling at Becanda's affection. "Yeah well that's becoming a special occasion in itself" Becanda replied.

"Yeah, sorry" said Tamara. Becanda waved her hand and said "oh don't be, we always knew that this would happen sooner or later, in our case it just happened sooner." Tamara pulled a confused face and said "you're really starting to mature, it's weird." Becanda laughed and replied "yeah, that's what happened when you stare at bits of wood all day" Becanda paused and then added "but I'd still rather do this than your job." "Damn!" Tamara shouted.

Becanda took a few steps towards Vana and gave her a hug saying "hello Mrs Vana, you're looking well." This was not the first time this had happened but Vana was still getting used to it, she stalled for a moment until her finally muttered "that's sweet" and pattered her on the back.

"So what are you making?" Vana asked when Becanda finally let go. "Oh, just a new dining table for Mr Uriah" she said with disinterest. "I am happy that you're hear but I can't play, I've got to finish this" She kicked plank of wood she had been planing. "No but we can keep you company" said Tamara. "Or you three could go find Hansad and spend the day together" Caltha said as she chiselled away small chips of wood. "But I need to get this done" Becanda argued. "Considering the circumstances I don't think anyone will mind much" Caltha replied. Becanda smiled and said "thanks mom." "You're welcome sweetie, have fun!" said Caltha.

Becanda went inside and got changed into something more colourful as Tamara and Vana waited outside the front door, they waited for some time. When Becanda finally emerged, she was wearing a pink dress, had completely different ribbons in her hair and Tamara was certain she had also had a wash. "I was beginning to think you got lost" Tamara said tapping the tip of her tail against the ground.

"I had to freshen up" Becanda responded shrugging her shoulders. "Oh I think we all know why" Tamara replied a sly smile on her face. Becanda blushed slightly and said "and what of it?" Tamara was disappointed, just last year Becanda would have screamed at her and denied everything, she was watching her friends grow up and part of her hated it.

"That's pretty rich coming from you missy" Vana said crossing her arms. Tamara looked at her and replied "what are you talking about?" "Oh you know, you and a certain crimson haired Cicindeli boy, one a couple years older than you" Vana answered, coping the smile Tamara had done earlier. Tamara face went crimson she turned around and said "you're delusional!" "Oh really I saw how you were gazing into his rainbow coloured eyes, you just wanted to fall into his arms didn't you" Vana said as she hugged herself, giving Becanda a live demonstration of what she was suggesting.

Becanda started to giggle and Tamara wheeled around, anger and frustration clearly visible in her every gesture and expression "do you really want to walk down this road Vana?" Tamara said. Vana being, well, aware of how terrifying she could be and knew what Tamara was talking about Vana back down "ok I'll leave it, for now" she replied.

Hansad and his father Adair were part of the team that cut down trees for timber. The village did not need a lot of new wood, they mostly recycled old pieces so the small group of woodcutters could see to everyone's needs.

They may have had to spend hours looking for Hansad fortunately both he and Becanda told each other everything and she knew exactly where he was. Up ahead they could hear axes clashing with wood and people shouting, above the roar they heard someone shout "Timber!" then there was a great crash as a tree hit the ground with a mighty thud.

When they finally arrived, they found ten people crawling over the fallen tree, hacking away at it. On the upper branched the could see Hansad cutting away the leaves and twigs "now don't faint with excitement" Tamara whispered to Becanda. She rolled her eyes and pushed Tamara away. Hansad was the same age as Becanda, with black hair and chitin.

One of the other foresters noticed the girls and pointed them out "Hansad your girlfriend's here!" He looked confused, it was rare when anyone came to see them, and gazed to where the woods woman had pointed, once he realised that she was not yanking his chain he buried his axe in the trunk and walked to his friends.

Once he was close enough he ran up to Becanda and hugged her, "we only saw each other this morning" She laughed hugging him back. "I know but I enjoy it" he replied. "Are you too going to do that all day?" Adair called out. "We can talk after I've finished removing the branches" he told them and hurried back to his dad while the girls sat down and talked.

Adair was not a Cicindeli like his son but a Lamia, whereas most Lamias were one colour and occasionally had a pattern running down their backs, Adair had a thick band of red scales followed by a thinner black section, this repeated all the way down to his tail. His hair was brown and his eyes were different colours one was yellow and the other a deep blue.

As to why his son was a Cicindeli was not as preposterous as it seemed, his mother was a Cicindeli. Any member of the different races could have children with any other, though there were a few rules, firstly it did seem to be a little more difficult to conceive though you could still have several children if you tried. Secondly the child would always be the same race as the mother.

Hansad worked like a man possessed and in record time he finished "someone wanted to impress" Tamara said as Hansad joined them. "Maybe I did, what of it?" Hansad replied. Tamara slapped her hands on the grass and said "oh you two aren't fun anymore, where's the blushing? Where's the squealing? Where's the begging me to stop?"

"Well maybe you should try something new" Becanda said. "But I had already planned the speech at your wedding, I was going to make you redder than a tomato" Tamara replied folding her arms. "Tamara, are you saying that you spent almost all of your free time thinking of ways to tease these two" Vana said wagging her finger between Becanda and Hansad. "Pretty much, yeah" Tamara nodded. Vana turned to Hansad and Becanda and told them "you could do a lot better you know." They two of them the started laughing.

Adair allowed Hansad to leave early and the four of them began to walk around the borders of the village, talking. Tamara once again explained why she was going on this trip, she gave out the usual ones but if she was honest there was another more personal reason. She was growing up, every day she had to deal with other people's problems and soon she would be so heavily depended upon that she would almost certainly never leave the village again.

This was her one chance to see the world, to know what was beyond her forest, just as Aarush, Vana and Samuel did and nothing would stop her.

Her friends were concerned, everyone knew that she would be travelling with Samuel, though no one dared do any more than mention it in passing. Tamara had always felt it was funny, Becanda and Hansad had known Samuel as long as she had, they had been there when Samuel had first dropped into their lives, he had even pulled them out of a burning building but they still refused to see the truth. They were still convinced that the old stories were true, that humans stole babied and ate people hearts, Tamara wondered what had allowed her to see the truth so easily? What made her so different?

Tamara reassured them that there was nothing to worry about and even if there was Vana was coming with her and she could beat a mountain into submission. The day passed quietly both Tamara and Vana both enjoyed the glacial pace of things. The sun started to set, Tamara and Hansad found the heat starting to leave her body, they had to return home. Becanda would make certain that Hansad would make it and Vana did the same for Tamara.

They went through the market; the villagers were packing up their products for the tomorrow. This was Vana favourite time of day the orange glow of the sun, the way everything started to slow down, the half-hearted chirps of the birds, that slight heaviness of her eyelids that made her feel warm inside, it was a magical moment.

Once they were outside Tamara home, Vana gave her a hug and waved her goodbye. Before heading home Vana decided to take short walk, give herself time to unwind.

She let her mind wander and she thought about how good her life was, how lucky she had been and how she wished her parents were still around to enjoy it with her. Her father had passed away when she was about six, there had been something nasty chasing them and they he had distracted it long enough for both her and her mother to escape. Her mom had died five years ago due to an illness, normally a Dingonek could fight of just about any disease but her mom had not eaten in a while and she had been to weak.

Even though they had nothing her parents had always done the best they could for her, always put Vana before everything else, she missed them and hoped wherever they were, they were happy.

The next thing Vana knew she was pushing open the door to her house. "That's weird" Vana whispered, she could not remember travelling here. Vana shrugged her shoulders and went inside.

The low light meant that it was difficult to see and she tripped over a pair of winter boots that Samuel had made for her, she was the only person other than Samuel who wore them. They were damn good boots, filled with wool and built to last, her feet had never been so warm while walking through the snow.

Vana stoked the fire sat down in her favourite chair and waited for bed time. This may have sounded boring and Samuel may very well have agreed but for someone like Vana it was quite possibly the most wonderful experience in the world. She would not be able to do this for a while so she savoured every moment of it.

The sun went down and it was time for bed, Vana put out the fire and lit a candle, this was specially made to provide the most amount of light possible, Vana had no idea how it worked but there was plenty of light to see by. As she Yawned Vana said "I'll sleep well tonight."

Chapter 3

It had been a grand send off, almost the entire village had turned up to wish them luck and secretly tell them not to go. In fact, Tamara was starting to think their plan was to keep them so distracted that they would be unable to leave. She put her tail down and with no small amount of wailing they left.

Surprisingly Pancha had decided to walk them to Samuel's home. Tamara had asked her if she was being serious and shockingly she said she was. "You've never wanted to go before, what's changed?" Tamara asked. "What's changed is that I'm going to be giving up my daughter for thirty days" replied Pancha. Her reply was firm but Tamara could tell she was nervous, it was not every day that you willing came face to face with a monster.

"Are you sure you're alright dear?" Pancha asked Vana she was referring to her rucksack, which was far larger than Tamara's. Vana smiled and said "yeah, to be honest I barely notice it plus I've been practicing." "I'm just concerned that you two won't have enough to eat" Pancha said. "Oh stop being such a worry wart, mom you know Vana a good hunter" Tamara said, she then paused and turned to Vana saying "there that's another thing you should be proud of."

Pancha had brought this up because Lamias did not eat every day, instead they had one large meal every week or so, an adult could pack away ten pounds of meat in one sitting. They were also strictly carnivorous, if a Lamia ate fruit or vegetables, in any significant quantities, they would experience stomach cramps, they could also have bowel problems and in rare cases develop ulcers.

They emerged from the forest to find Samuel sitting outside his cave, resting his back against the mountain, with his eyes shut. Pancha stopped in her tracks and just stared at him, she had only met him once before, back when the village had first found out where he lived, it had almost ended badly until Samuel had shamed them all by making them realise how much they were hurting Tamara. "Are you ok?" Tamara whispered taking hold of her mother hand. "Yeah, let's go" Pancha replied.

Samuel was rolling his head around, singing a song none of them had heard before and in a language, they could not recognise. He was so focused on this that he did not hear the three of the approach. Samuel did not have the voice of a nightingale and feeling a little sick welling up Vana gave him a gentle kick.

He was not startled, he calmly opened his eyes and said "what took you so long?" "We had to claw our way out of the village, through wild dogs and angry hornets" Tamara explained. Samuel raised an eyebrow. "Oh fine! We got hugs and kisses from our friends and family" Tamara replied. "My heart bleeds for you" said Samuel.

Out of the corner of his eye Samuel noticed something, something that appeared to be another Tamara but when he looked he found something far more shocking. He was silent for over a minute just staring at Pancha, who was feeling disturbed by his gaze, trying to be certain that he was not hallucinating. When Samuel was certain he was not he said "Hello Pancha, this is a surprise." He paused and then added "not an unpleasant one, mind you."

Pancha did not reply she just continued staring "I don't bite" Samuel said. Tamara stood beside her mom, nudged her with her elbow and said "mom say something." Pancha was snapped for her stupor and mumble out "hello."

"Haven't seen you in a while, how have you been?" Samuel asked as he stood up and stretched. "Umm good" Pancha replied. "Marvellous" Samuel said clapping his hands and added "but I must ask why are you here?" "How do you know I'm not just here to see my daughter off?" Pancha responded. He smiled and told her "because by the amount you're shaking there is no way you are here for a heartfelt goodbye."

She looked confused and said "from what Tamara told me you shouldn't be able to read my body language." Tamara then interrupted and explained "no I said he found it more difficult, not that he Couldn't do it."

Pancha took a deep breath and said "look I want to know why you are doing this?" Samuel replied "I thought those two already explained it" pointing his fingers at Tamara and Vana. "They told me why they were doing it but I want to know your reason" Pancha clarified.

Samuel gave this some thought and then told her "I want to see what's over the next hill." "Ok but why?" said Pancha. He shrugged his shoulder and said "there is no why." Pancha was silent as she let his answer swirl around in her head and they gave her as much time as she needed. "That doesn't make any sense" Pancha said after a minute. Samuel could not argue; it did not make any sense to leave his comfortable life for a month of living rough just to see the sights, "Human nature" Samuel replied with a smile.

"Don't worry you get used to it" Vana told Pancha, patting her shoulder. "Ok now do you have any other questions, I don't mind answering them" Samuel said cheerfully, it was nice having someone new to talk to. Pancha was still nervous, it was proving difficult to completely ignore all those frightening stories her mom had told her when she was a child but she was beginning to see what her daughter kept telling her.

There was nothing threating in his movements, words or face, it was just as Tamara had said he was just a person, no different from her. Even so she would prefer that he stay a few steps away for now.

Pancha asked many personal questions, most of which Samuel answered truthfully they were a few however which were far to private to answer. With each one he answered both Tamara and Vana could see that Pancha was becoming more and more relaxed. Samuel explained how he got here or more accurately that he had no idea how he got here, he explained how he knew about the crops last year as well as the solution.

By the end of the probing Pancha had become very interested in Samuel and his life but Tamara and Vana were becoming anxious to get going and they explained that if they did not leave soon they would only get a few miles before they had to set up camp. "Thank you Pancha" Samuel said. "For what?" Pancha asked. "For giving me a chance" Samuel explained.

Pancha then began to chuckle at how pig headed she had been these past few years. She then took a deep breath and said "Samuel, there is something I should have told you since the day of the fire." "What's that?" he asked. "I am sorry for the way we have treated you" Pancha paused and then added "above all else, thank you for saving my daughters life." "You don't…" Samuel said but Pancha cut him off "No this has been a long time coming and you deserve it and so I say it again thank you Samuel." Realising that would not end otherwise Samuel said "You're welcome."

Tamara and Vana were smiling this was better than they could have hoped, it may very well take a few more years but it had been their goal to get Samuel into the village and now it was closer than ever. Pancha turned away from Samuel and proceeded to smother Tamara in hugs and kisses.

As Tamara struggled to break free, Pancha made her promise that she would be safe and not take any unnecessary risk. Pancha did the same with Vana though there was less kissing and finally Pancha turned back to Samuel and told him to be careful. "Always" Samuel replied.

The day was moving on and they could not stay any longer, so with a tap on Vana and Tamara's shoulder he told them it was time to go. Pancha did not follow but she did wave and Tamara did the same until she was out of sight.

"Nervous?" Samuel asked. "A little but my excitement is overpowering it" Tamara said. "I more annoyed that I won't be able to sleep in my big soft bed" Vana answered. Samuel smiled and said "it's not all bad you can use Tamara as a pillow, though she lumpy." Tamara stared at Samuel with eyes like daggers and said "I am not lumpy!" "So you don't mind being used as a pillow, excellent" Samuel replied with a cheeky grin. Tamara was left speechless as she tried to think of a response but Vana intervened and said "I'm not going to all the trouble of hauling around this stuff and not use it" she pointed to her rucksack.

The walked past an apple tree and took a few moments to pull a couple of the fruit down. She shared one of them with Samuel and the two enjoyed a nice mid-morning snack. They were lovely, with an exquisite texture and just the right level of sweetness.

The old mountain shrunk steadily until it disappeared entirely to reveal a colossal lake, surrounded by a picturesque beach. Without the cover of the mountain and combined with the cool lake water the breeze became much chiller. While Samuel found this to be a welcome relief Tamara was grumbling, she preferred it when it was muggy and at least thirty-five degrees Celsius.

"You could always put a sweater on, help trap the heat" Samuel said. For Tamara and those like her putting on more layers was not as simple a strategy as it would have been for Samuel or a Boreray. As she was cold blooded, her temperature was entirely dependent on her environment, so putting on more clothes would not store up heat, it would only insulate that which was already there, not to mention that most of her body was composes of a giant tail.

None the less it was the best she could do so the three of them stopped for a moment while Tamara put on a yellow goat's wool jumper with a black diamond in the centre. "Better?" Vana asked. Tamara wriggled slightly, she could no longer feel the breeze on her torso, sapping her warmth away, "not perfect but an improvement" Tamara replied.

While Tamara had been sorting herself out Samuel took the time to examine the beauty of his environment, it was indeed difficult to put into words just how magical it was, Samuel was even thinking of inventing a new word to describe it. The sun reflected of the crystal-clear waters made it seem as if the lake was made from crystal, the sand was almost pure white, the air was so fresh each breath filled him with euphoria.

"If your finished ogling the lake can we get moving?" Tamara said poking him in the back. "You know the whole living in an enchanted forest thing as really left you blind to the beauty of the world" Samuel replied "if you had spent time in a car fume infested city, filled with those concrete and glass abominations they called buildings you'd be just as inspired as I am." Tamara looked at him and said "well you are inspiring me to strap you to a log and drag you along, now move." Samuel snorted and mumbled "kids today don't know notin about notin."

About a mile further on Tamara stopped and looked at the ground. "What's the matter?" Asked Samuel. "It's just this is the farthest I have ever been away from the village" Tamara explained. "But we have always been pushing the limit, just last week we got here" Samuel reasoned. "I know that but I also knew I would be sleeping in my own bed the same night" Tamara said "I guess I've just realised that I won't see my mom for a "month" as you call it. "We can always go back" Samuel said. Tamara shook her head and said "no, this is my last chance and I'm going to take it."

Despite the conviction in her voice Tamara had still not moved. Samuel knew exactly what to do, he stood beside Tamara and held out his hand. She stared at it and then with a smile took it. "One, two three" Samuel counted and the pair of them took the first step.

Roughly an hour later Tamara called for the three of them to stop, she sat down on the sand and pulled out some of her writing supplies, and a specially prepared piece of paper, it was filled with a series of squares, like graph paper. Each square represented about an hour's walking, Samuel had thought of it.

Of course, without a time keeping device and a camera with unlimited storage space Samuel could not have hoped to fill it in himself but thanks to Tamara's and

Vana's excellent memory, this allowed them to fill it in with remarkable accuracy.

While those got started on that Samuel began to scan the tree line and the water for any plants or animals he had not seen before. So, close to home he did not expect much unless this lake was the size of the Mediterranean but as his old lecturer once said "you find the greatest number of species in the place you study the most."

He could hear some woodpigeons, cooing away in the distance, he had already done a piece on them but still he had always enjoyed the sound they made. He stared at the sharp cut of point between the sand and the grass, as if someone had drawn a line on the earth and said "right the forest stays on that side and the beach on this one!"

"Come on time a wasting" Vana said tapping him on his shoulder. The two of them finished and anxious to continue. Every so often Samuel would look behind and see the old mountain, his home grow smaller, it was taller than he gave it credit for as he could still see it, even after they had covered over ten miles.

The beach and forest continued to stretch out into the distance and the three of them started to receive a new appreciation as to just how big their forest was. "Vana have you ever been this way?" Samuel asked. She shook her head and said "no I came form that away" she pointed deeper into the forest "about a three-week's journey and you come so a mountain range, I climbed them to get here and I have told you all this before."

Samuel tried to remember but he could not "did you?" he asked quizzically. "Yes, although just as I was starting to explain a hare jumped out in front of us and you rushed off to document it" Vana explained. Samuel smiled and said "well I'd love to hear it now."

"Yes tell us again" Tamara said excitedly. "Well the mountain that separates the land is tall, so tall the tip always had snow on it" Vana explained. "There is a village on its slopes, home to harpies and Pteromy, a strange place where you have to fly or glide to get from one house to another."

"Once you reach the bottom, you see a huge ocean of grass, as far as the eye can see, it is filled with animals unlike any found in the forest, they get huge, some of them as tall as trees" said Vana.

This got Samuel's attention and he started to ask her about all the animals she had ever seen. From her descriptions, he was confident she was talking about elephants, giraffes and rhinos. The grasslands were most likely a savannah. Yet there was more, creatures that, from the sound of it, belonged in a fantasy novel, lizards with colossal necks, giant birds, with no wings and teeth that ate meat.

"I also encountered a village there, it was like ours but it had a huge wooden wall around it to keep the animals out" Vana continued. The village had been home to Ogres, Cyclopes, Minotaurs, Satyrs and the Cento, a race of lizard people and the moment they had spotted Vana they had chased her off.

Samuel took out a piece of paper and jotted down the names of all the creatures she had seen, though some of them held no meaning to him. He would not be adding them to his book however, it was not because he did not believe Vana, Samuel did accept that these creatures existed. It was without seeing them in person Tamara could not draw a picture and Samuel was unable to study them.

Then Samuel realised something that conflicted with her story "wait when we first met you told us you came from this way" he pointed to the ground. Vana shook her head and told him "no I crossed the mountains, walked through the forest and I came out further down there" she pointed towards the old mountain. "I did not tell you about the trip when we first met because I was still a little unsure about you and when I wasn't any more you didn't bring it up again, until now" she added. Samuel rubbed his chin and said "that's fair."

Travelling was thirsty work, fortunately they had a huge water source nearby, so Samuel, took of his boots, socks and greaves, rolled up his trousers kneeled in the cold water and stuck his face below the surface, taking in great gulps. When he finally pulled his head out of the water Tamara said "you do realise that you will be going to the toilet all day?" Samuel shrugged his shoulders and said "do have any idea how great this water is, it's like drinking nectar."

The dip had the added benefit of keeping him cool, even with the breeze it was still hot. Vana obviously agreed with him because a few moments later she did the same. "You know at times like this I'm glad I'm cold blooded" Tamara said. "Yeah well after the sun goes down we will still be able to move about so don't get to cocky" Samuel replied. "True but when you go to bed you will be tossing and turning because of the heat, while I have wonderful dreams" Tamara said smugly. Samuel squinted and said "you win this round Tamara."

The sun would be setting soon, so they set up camp. The unpacked the tents, a larger one for Tamara and Vana and a single for Samuel. The built a fire in the centre, and Samuel began to cook their dinner, Tamara would not be partaking it was still a few days to her next meal.

Vana pulled out some preserved chicken and Samuel placed it one the frying pan. "There we go, that should make it nice and crispy." Discreetly he pulled a small package from his pack "So Vana what would go well this that?" he asked. Vana was busy talking with Tamara about what they would do tomorrow she looked at the frying meat and said "well a fresh salad would be nice" and the turned away.

Samuel smiled and said "yeah but we don't have that so what else?" he carefully undid the bundle. "Well some black trumpets but..." as Vana spoke Samuel revealed the horn of plenty mushrooms "No you haven't!" Vana yelled as she grabbed the package from him "Samuel you crafty devil!" "I thought you'd like that" Samuel said cheerfully.

As Vana enjoyed her tea, Samuel looked out at the setting sun, it an astounding sight. "Well not a bad way to end the first day" Samuel said. Tamara nodded and said "yep." "Got anything more insightful to add?" Samuel asked. Tamara looked at him and said "could you do any better?" Samuel chuckled and said "probably not." Behind them Vana made a little squeal and Tamara added "though I think she has found something she loves more."

The sun vanished on the horizon and the air began to cool. Though by Samuel standards it would be warm all night, for Tamara it was no longer hot enough to maintain active. She yawned and rubbed her eyes "maybe you should go to bed" Samuel said. Tamara shook her head and replied "no I want to see the stars before I go to bed, I rarely get to see them." Samuel had an idea as to why she was doing this, before the trip he had often talked about sleeping under the stars.

"Well if you're going to do that you might want to come a little closer to the fire" Samuel said and Tamara, with a little help from Vana did so. She perked up a bit and her tail ran all around the circumference of the fire. "If you get any bigger your bed is going to collapse under your weight" said Samuel. "No it won't, it's specially made" Tamara replied.

It started to get dark and usually they would have gone to bed by now even Samuel and Vana started to yawn. Samuel looked up and through the clouds Samuel could make out a few twinkling lights. "Tamara" Samuel said, pointing to the sky.

She looked up at them and said nothing for over fifteen minutes, she just stared at them. Samuel and Vana copied her and enjoyed the simple pleasure of star gazing. "What are they?" Tamara asked. "They're stars" Vana replied. "I know that but "What" are they?" Tamara clarified. "They're massive balls of nuclear plasma" Samuel answered.

The spell was broken on Tamara and Vana and they looked at Samuel, still appreciating the sky and said together "what?" Samuel looked at them and realised that he had over complicated things again, he had a habit of doing that "well what they are suns, just very far away" he replied and then added "the sun is a star it's just very close up."

"How many are there?" Vana asked. Samuel smiled and told her "more than you could count in thousand lifetimes."

Samuel stretched and said "well I'm knackered, goodnight you two." They wished him a good night and watched as he vanished into his tent. A few minutes later they followed suit, inside the tent, they got changed. Tamara looked at Vana tail and asked "You're not going to sting me by accident?" "No, I have to want to sting someone for the venom to come out" she reassured her.

Tamara was asleep in moments and Vana followed soon after, enjoying the sound of the waves lapping against the sand "life is good" Vana mumbled.

Chapter 4

Samuel was beginning to wonder if this forest had an end, they had been travelling for three days and the tree line remained unbroken. "Oh well maybe today will be different" Samuel said as wriggled under his blankets wondering if he should get up.

The first night out had been a little tough, he always had a little trouble getting sleep in a new place but he had finally gotten used to it. He could see the sunlight through the walls of his tent, he decided it was better to get an early start.

Samuel removed his night shirt and got dressed, he remembered that Tamara would be eating tomorrow, so they needed to find something large to hunt by then, most likely a deer. Not a big problem, Vana was a good hunter and she had brought her bow.

He popped his head out of the tent and shuddered in the cool, he really wanted to snuggle up until the air got warmer but that was loser talk, so Samuel stepped outside. No one else was up yet, Samuel started the fire and packed away his tent, after several minutes of groaning the job was done.

Filling a bowl with lake water Samuel brushed his teeth and had a shave. Funnily enough the toothbrush had been one thing he did not need the re-invent, the villagers had been making and using them for longer than any of them could remember, which was saying something. As for his razor, Samuel had found a lump of obsidian, a black volcanic glass, he had no idea how it got there but he wasn't complaining. The good thing about obsidian was that it carried a wicked edge and this let him get a very close shave.

Samuel took some eggs and began to fry them alongside a few strips of Kangaroo bacon, which Samuel had never heard of until he had shown up in this world. As the smell started to drift through their camp and Samuel enjoyed a nice cup of pulpy juice, Vana emerged from her tent.

She had clearly just gotten out of bed as her hair was trying to escape from her scalp, he brought it back into line. "Did you sleep well?" Samuel asked as he turned the meat. "I had a lovely dream" Vana said, Samuel smiled and then she added "until I was woken up by what I think was braying camel" Vana started to imitate Samuel packing his things away. "Samuel frowned and said "you keep that up and you're not having any." Vana stopped and chuckled.

Samuel plated up her breakfast alongside a cup of juice and they ate. As Samuel looked over at the horizon he saw something odd, he tapped Vana with his foot and said "that island, was it there yesterday?" Still chewing her eggs Vana followed Samuel's finger and scanned the water. He was right, there was an island in the distance, it was small just a spec really, most likely miles away but it was defiantly there.

She shrugged and said "well we probably just didn't notice it yesterday; we were pretty tired." Samuel nodded that was probably what had happened, and it gave Tamara something to do before they set off.

Samuel, who had seen some new species in the past two days continued where he left of yesterday. He was currently writing down about little owls and had filled three pages of facts in under a day. Vana on the other hand enjoyed a spot of sun bathing.

As the day began to get warmer Tamara began to stir in her tent and just as Vana and Samuel were packing away the plates and cup. She emerged ready for the day ahead, when Samuel explained the island on the horizon she made a little mark on her drafts as a reminder, she said there was little point adding it if they had no idea how large or where exactly it was.

"What do you need a reminder for? You can remember what do wore, on this day five years ago" Samuel said. "Navy blue top" Tamara said "but that's not the point, I may remember it but until you brought it up it was still lodged in the back of my mind."

Tamara was allowed a few minutes to finish waking up, they also passed her a cup of hot water with a small amount of lemon peel. When she said she was ready, the group picked up their rucksacks and continued their journey.

"Another fine day" Vana said as they walked along the beach. "Can't argue with that" Samuel replied "and I must say Tamara you have been doing extremely well" he added. Tamara, having spent her entire life under a canopy usually had some difficulty with open spaces, she just preferred the security offered by buildings and trees but she had only complained once so far. "Yeah well I'm with friends so it's not so bad" said Tamara.

As they pushed on Samuel noticed that the lakeshore was different. The sand had an undulating pattern to it, as if the water was pulling it towards something. Samuel quickly learned what, up ahead the forest stopped, and a huge river barred the way.

It was big, one of the widest he had ever seen, easily a mile across, he could make out the shore in the distance and what was more surprising was, the distinct lack of large trees. "What do we do now?" Tamara asked. She was right this was a puzzler, there was no way Tamara could swim across that, it was far too cold and even if the water was conveniently heated to body temperature, the current was far too strong. Samuel supposed the only one who had a hope of making it across would be Vana.

From where the three of them were standing it looked impossible, but they all knew from past experience that what something looks like and what it is are two different things. Samuel suggested that they follow the river until they find a bridge but both the girls shot it down, no one could build a bridge strong enough for a river that wide.

Realising they were going nowhere, they set up camp beside the riverbank. Samuel quickly came up with an idea, they could build a boat, well more of a raft and row across. This was a good plan and the girls nodded their approval. There was however on small flaw, none of them knew how to build a raft.

Vana then said "it's never stopped us before." Samuel and Tamara smiled and he said "well you've certainly got us there." Vana took out an axe and started to chop down a few trees while Samuel and Tamara worked on the plans. They used a tried and tested formula, Samuel would produce the rough idea and Tamara would make the sketches presentable and easy to understand.

To get a rough idea of how big it would need to be to support all three of them and their gear, Samuel drew rectangle in the sand. He asked Tamara to sit in it and guess the raft would need to be three metres by four to fit them all in comfortably. "Why do you have to grow so big, you're only thirteen?" Samuel asked with faked annoyance. "I dunno why are you so small your already twenty-three?"

Behind them they heard a tree falling to the ground "she made short work of that" Samuel said looking at an imaginary watch. "Why are you looking at your wrist?" Tamara asked. "Err it's just a human thing" Samuel replied, not wanting to get bogged down in how humans measured time, he would tell her another day, today they had work to do.

He went over to Vana and used his forearm as a rudimentary measuring device, Vana had picked a good tree, tall put not very thick, "and you keep saying you don't do anything" Samuel said patting her on the back. "I haven't it just made sense to chop down this tree" she replied pointing at the wood, with her crimson finger. "Not me, I would have tried to chop down some giant, forgetting that we don't have any saws big enough to handle them" Samuel replied. "Well I can't argue with that" Vana replied with a smile

Vana went on to find more suitable trees while Samuel and Tamara removed all the branches and leaves. The day wore on and the group had gathered five trunks from their size they assumed they would need about ten to twelve more. "Break time" Tamara said and she put away her knife.

Samuel was the last one to the camp site and he was dragging a piece of timber. "What you got that for?" Vana asked. "Are you going to make a lovely statue of me?" Tamara said running her fingers through her hair. "No, we are going to need oars so I'm starting on this one" Samuel explained.

He took out his machete and started to create the rough shape of the oar. He became extremely focused on his job so much so that he did not notice Tamara and Vana leave to continue their work. The next thing he knew the fire had been started and their tea was cooking.

He had made good progress, the first one was almost complete and the girls told him that they had cut down and prepared another seven logs. They also provided Samuel with another two lengths of wood and told him that he should just focus on them tomorrow. Vana passed over his tea, Vana had shot down a few ducks and had prepared a simple stew.

He finished his tea and started putting the finishing touches to the oar, for this he used his knife rather than a machete. "I don't understand why you won't let me get you a new one" said Tamara. "It holds sentimental value" Samuel replied. "I know that, but just because I get you a new knife doesn't mean you have to throw that one away" Tamara responded. "I shall keep using this blade until it doth shatter in five score shards" Samuel said like an Elizabethan country gent.

By the time the sun went down Samuel had finished, it was a decent job for a first effort. He had even worked in a comfort grip. With the last few minutes of sunlight Samuel sharpened his knife for the next day.

Vana and Samuel got an early start the next day even Tamara was pushing herself and was up long before Samuel could have thought. The girls went off to find the final trees and Samuel worked on the last two paddles, he supposed he should be able to finish them before sundown.

As his machete peeled flakes of barks from the stump Samuel looked out over the water, the island was there, closer than it had been yesterday. "Must have travelled further than we thought" he mumbled. He could make out a few details, it had trees on it, though he was uncertain how large they were and he wasn't sure but it looked like it a second piece of land beside it, though that could just be a trick of the water.

Behind him he could hear the girl dragging the logs to the river side. "Hey Samuel where do you suppose the water goes?" asked Tamara. "Hmm" Samuel replied. "Samuel pay attention!" Tamara shouted. He was snapped out of his trance and said "sorry what did you say?" "The water, it's flowing away from the lake right, so where does it go?" she repeated.

"Well it either flows into a completely different lake, further down or it goes out to sea" he answered. "Really the sea?" Tamara said. Samuel shrugged and said "possibly, why do you want to sail down there?" he gestured with his machete further down river. "Yes I do but not today" Tamara replied "maybe another time" she added.

The girls took the rope from out of the bags and lashed the logs together, behind country girls they knew a thing or two about knots. By the half way point something became obvious, they did not have enough rope. No matter however, there was a solution nearby, Tamara went to a nearby willow tree and began to peel the bark from the trunk while Vana prepared the pot, they would boil the bark for about fifteen minutes, then make their own rope.

Tamara kept bringing more and more bark while Vana quickly process it, producing metres of rope. It was a setback, they would not be leaving today but no one cared, they still had plenty of time.

By sunset they had made excellent progress, Vana had gone to find something to Tamara to eat, she had been gone a while and should not be much longer. Just about the same moment Tamara began to feel hungry Vana returned with a young buck over her shoulders.

Both Vana and Tamara were big believers in nose to tail eating, and they wanted to tuck into the organs, where all the flavour was. Samuel was more than happy to let them have it and settled for the lean leftovers found on the legs.

Samuel prepared a range of dishes, form steaks to stews. Though both Samuel and Vana could pack it away when they were hungry, none of them even came close to Tamara, she ate over half of the deer in a single meal. Tamara had no molars, she could not chew so instead she swallowed her food whole.

With her stomach almost filled to bursting point Tamara slid into the tent without a word and was fast asleep in moments, she would not move again till at least tomorrow afternoon and that was being optimistic.

This was of no concern the other two as they had planned for it and they could spend tomorrow perfecting the raft so that it did not break apart in the middle of the river.

When Vana woke up the next morning she discovered, once again, that Samuel had woken up first. He had his trousers rolled up, was standing knee deep in the lakes water and he was holding his walking stick. Attached to the end was his knife and he was poised to strike at something in the water. Vana understood he was catching their breakfast.

Vana spent a few moments watching him stand motionless, like a statue. He was not much to look at, he always looked like he was ill, but he did seem to possess a confidence, charm and intelligence that more than made up for it. She found that she enjoyed watching him work, her heartbeat went up a few beats and her cheeks went ever so slightly red.

Then Samuel struck, his spear plunged through the water and when he lifted it above his head Vana could see a good-sized fish wriggling at the end. Samuel quickly put the poor thing out of its misery and Vana climbed out of the tent. Behind her Tamara said, half slurred "don't do anything naughty while I'm out of commission!"

"It's your imagination that most concerns me" Vana replied and let Tamara snooze. "How many so far?" Vana asked. "Four" Samuel replied removing the knife from the specially carved hollow at the top of his walking stick and ensured it was bone dry before placing it back, he did not want his knife to rust. Samuel had been planning to make a tip of bone or antler and thus remove the problem all together but he had never gotten around to it. If he had time tonight, he might give it a go.

As they were eating breakfast Vana gave out a small cry of pain. When Samuel looked up he saw her rooting around her own mouth and pulled out a tooth. It was a fearsome thing, like a great white sharks'. Without a second thought she threw the tooth away, like a shark Vana went through several sets in a year. "You ok?" Samuel asked. She waved her hand and replied "I've been losing teeth since I was one year old." She scooped another piece of fish into her mouth and said "I do…" "Don't talk with your mouth full!" Samuel said. Vana swallowed and then repeated "I do wish sometimes that I had the same teeth all my life." "Well think of it this way, in fifty years you will still be able to eat steak" Samuel replied. "You got a point there" she said.

With breakfast behind them Vana went back to finishing the raft and Samuel put the finishing touches to the final oar.

Once it was done he took two of the oars to the to the raft and assisted Vana. Vana pulled the final knot tight and it was done. They hammered a stake into the sand tied a strong rope to both it and the raft and pushed it into the river. The river tugged on the rope but could not pull the it free.

They stood on the raft and it sunk ever so slightly into the water but the two of them were still bone dry. Vana did a quick jump, to simulate something going wrong and the raft bobbed up and down but stayed above the water. "Not bad" Samuel said.

An idea popped into his head, maybe at some point he could build a boat and maybe a small pier on the lakeshore, near his home, that should keep him busy for a few months.

The raft was done, it was not an attractive thing but it looked sturdy enough and it only had to make one trip plus the river may be fast but it was not rough. They pulled the raft back onto the shore.

The pair of them had the rest of the day free, they could do a bit of exploring but it just did not seem fair on Tamara, so they milled around camp, Samuel used the antlers from the deer Vana caught to carve a new tip for his walking stick/spear.

Vana sighed, she had nothing to do, she had hoped that the raft would have taken up more of the day. "Still haven't found a hobby?" Samuel said. "No" Vana replied.

"You could try pressing flowers" Samuel answered. "Pressing flowers?" Vana asked quizzically. "Why not? You've rejected everything else" Samuel answered.

She tapped her foot and stinger on the sand "you got me there" said Vana. She began to look at the flowers that grew around the trees, she picked out some good examples of orchids, daffodils, roses and bluebells. It did seem like a shame to use the paper for just a test run but Samuel reassured her that he did not mind.

While Vana gave her potential hobby a try Samuel blew some dust off his carving. He looked across at her and noticed that she had not thrown in the towel yet, all other hobbies had bored her by now. "Maybe we've found a keeper?" Samuel thought. For now, he gave her all the time and space she needed.

By tea time, Vana was still fetching new flowers and pressing them, she had become so focused that, astonishingly, she did not notice that the food was ready. Samuel called to her and Vana was snapped out of her trance. "Enjoying yourself?" Samuel asked passing her a plate. "Yes, I think I'll keep it up" Vana replied cheerfully. "Well don't expect to do much of it while we're out here"

Samuel told her. "Yeah, yeah" Vana replied taking a bite of her meal.

At night Vana crawled back into her tent and yawned, placing her pressed flowers in the corner of her tent. Tamara was wake but it was clear she was still sleepy, she gently flicked her tail and asked "have a good day?" Vana got changed and replied "yeah, think I've finally found a hobby." "Oh, you've finally kissed him" Tamara said with a smile. "No, I've started collecting flowers" Vana corrected her. Tamara did not answer she was asleep again, "I'll tell you in the morning" Vana added as she lay down on her mattress.

It was mid-day before Tamara finally hauled herself out of bed, she was still groggy but she could at least move. "You know you're really getting fat Tamara" Samuel said poking at the meal still in her stomach. "Don't do that, unless you want to be covered in it" Tamara replied in no mood for jokes.

They put away the camp and placed all their things on the raft. They pushed the raft into the water and helped Tamara on, making certain she did not touch the cold water. Using their oars Samuel and Van pushed of from the bank.

The river was fast and it was difficult, even for Vana, to fight the current. Tamara suggested that they not bother, just focus on getting across and walk the back to the lake. It was a good plan, Samuel wondered why he hadn't thought of it.

The opposite shore got closer and Samuel could make out what type of habitat it was, a scrub forest. He stared to get excited, who knew what lived there, what new animals and plants he would find. He started to bounce and in the process rocked the raft "Samuel stop it!" The girls shouted worried that he would knock the supplied over board.

"Sorry" Samuel replied and controlled himself, he had not felt this way in so long, not since the first time he had gone on a research trip. He could still remember it, it had taken place in the Mediterranean and he spent two weeks documenting populations of the local wildlife in northern Italy, it had been magical, well for him at least most of his colleagues thought getting drunk in Malcesine was the height of pleasure.

The river had carried them over half a mile downstream before the got close to land but they had not encountered any crocodiles, so that was good. Samuel saw something move in the corner of his eyes, he looked at it and by the riverbank was a bird. It was big at first Samuel thought it was and Emu but no it was far too large, "an ostrich maybe" Samuel whispered. He then shook his head, no it had feathers covering his head and neck and it was still too big.

Then an idea struck him "no!" Samuel whispered "no! no! no!" he repeated, that would be impossible, then again, he was friends with a snake girl and a whatever Vana was. The raft hit the shore when he finally excepted that his eyes were telling the truth at which point he squealed.

Tamara and Vana leapt out of their skin, they had not known he could produce a sound like that.

"MOA!" Samuel shouted at the top of his voice. "What?" Tamara said but Samuel had already leapt of the raft and was making a bee line for the birds. He stomped through the water, ignoring the calls from his friends and any sense of caution.

There were five of them, two were drinking from the lake, the others were scratching in the sand looking for something. Samuel was unsure if this was a family or if they had just conveniently shown up in the same place and they were big. They stood as tall as an African elephant over three and a half metres covering in downy feather, with big powerful legs.

The Moas themselves were not particularly bothered, they showed curiosity at the little thing that had come out of the water, the smallest one even gave him a quick nibble. After which they went back about their business.

Samuel was enthralled by their every movement, he had dreamed about seeing them ever since he had seen a picture in an old text book. He had longed for scientists to do something about but had never held out much hope and yet here they were, back from the grave.

"Samuel, what are you doing?" Vana said grabbing him and wheeled him around. He had the biggest grin of his life etched into his face, his eyes were tearing up with joy and he pointed at the nearest bird and garbled the word "Moa."

Vana did admit they were impressive birds but they were certainly nothing to go mad about "I know you like animals but you're going a bit potty" she said. "You don't understand where I'm from Moa were extinct, there weren't any left and here they are" Samuel explained doing a little dance.

"We can spend all day looking at them if you want but first we need to get sorted" Vana said gesturing to the raft and their things. Samuel fidgeted not wanting to leave the animals in case they left but it was unfair to burden them just so he could enjoy himself so he dashed to the raft and helped Tamara unload.

In record time, all the supplies were unloaded and the raft disassembled, they dragged the logs into the scrubland in case they had to turn back. When Samuel returned two of the birds had left but the other three were still around and Samuel realised what they were doing, there were collecting gizzard stones, to help them digest their food.

Samuel began dotting down every minute detail, how they stood, how they interacted with each other. He saw they ate the leaves and branches from the nearby shrubs, their beaks were impressive slicing straight through fibrous twigs like shears.

He felt daring so he put his paper down and slowly approached the largest bird, it kept its eye on him but was otherwise unfazed. He was now standing directly beside the bird, its head towered above him. Samuel reached out his hand and touched the Moa, its skin twitched and the soft feathers felt amazing in his palm. As the bird's heat flowed into his hand Samuel chuckled, this was one of the greatest moments of his life.

The Moa got bored and walked off and Samuel returned to his work, one by one the other birds left, they had things they needed to do. Samuel would have loved to follow by they had a plan and he intended to stick to it.

"If all those birds were gone in your world how come you knew about them?" Tamara asked. "We found their bones and egg shells and scientist put the pieces together both figuratively and literally" Samuel explained "who knows maybe we will find a few fossils out there" he added.

"What's a fossil?" asked Vana. Samuel scratched the back of his neck and replied "well simply put a fossil is just an imprint left by a living thing, this could be a footprint, their bones, or their leavings." "And some humans spent their time looking at them?" Vana asked confused. "Oh no, they dedicated their entire lives to it" Samuel clarified.

With the distraction of the Moa removed Samuel took in his surroundings, it looked far more natural than the forest they had just left, the plants grew in a less organised fashion, the few trees that dotted the place rarely grew taller than the birds that lived there. It was also far more open, some sections had nothing but grass or small shrubs.

Samuel noticed that Tamara was holding herself "are you ok?" Samuel asked putting his arm around her. Tamara fidgeted and then replied "I'll be fine I just need to get used to it." He rubbed her arm and smiled, the trio sat down by the river they would wait as long as Tamara needed.

Chapter 5

Tamara was still having some trouble in the scrub forest but she was much improved. Samuel on the other hand had almost fainted with excitement when he realised just how many different creatures lived here. He had become so occupied that he had slowed the entire expedition to a crawl, in the past three days that had only covered about ten miles.

Both Tamara and Vana knew that the main point of this trip was to document species but this was getting ridiculous. Tamara had been drawing so much that she was getting cramps in her wrist.

They decided to hold a little intervention, they sat Samuel down who had been focused writing observations about a millipede he found on a branch. "Samuel, we understand you enjoy zoology but you're starting to slide into obsession" Tamara explained. "No, I'm not" Samuel replied with a smile.

Vana pinched the bridge of her nose and said "you've written over forty pages in three days, you've already dipped into my supply." "Look if you keep going like this, we will spend the entire trip sitting right here" Tamara said pointing at the ground.

Samuel looked through his work and saw the large stack of pages, he had been writing so quickly that a lot of the words were smudged and almost illegible. He said "you may have a point." He agreed that he should go easy on the writing and they made up for lost time.

It was difficult, he had to fight the urge to write about every new creature he saw but he kept his promise and tried to think about other things. "This place is weird" Tamara said. "What do you mean?" asked Vana. "Well it's the plants they look like they have all just grown wherever they could fit, there's no order to it" explained Tamara.

Samuel said "no, I've kept telling you that the forest is the strange thing, it's to organised, like someone planted it."

Tamara had heard Samuel explain that for years but she had never been able to visualise it, it had always seen so impossible and yet here it was. "It doesn't feel right" Tamara said. "Now you know how I felt" Samuel said patting her on the head.

It was a good point however, why was this place so natural and the forest so artificial? Samuel had long believed that both the forest and his cavern were made by people, who and why were far more difficult to answer but it was just to organised to be anything else.

So, if they had the ability to engineer a forest to grow in perfect synch and carve through a mountain, then why had they just stopped at that river, zoning laws perhaps? Samuel tussled his hair and thought "this place is so annoying, why can't I find a plaque that says this forest was planted by so and so in the year five thousand or whatever."

Samuel looked out over the water, in an attempt, to clear his head, the island was still visible unfortunately it was still too far away for Tamara to include it in her maps, that were coming along nicely.

The beach however was the one constant, it still stretched on ahead, pure white like fallen snow and gorgeous to behold. They had a break beside a small stream that flowed into the lake, Vana and Samuel took a light snack from a walnut tree they had found just a few minutes earlier.

Without a nutcracker, the seeds seemed impenetrable but both Vana and Samuel had their own solutions to this problem. Vana moved her hand out of the way and from an opening in her arm came a long claw. It was a fearsome thing twenty centimetres long yet it was more like a tooth than a nail, it was completely smooth around sides but the end was sharpened to a wicked point.

Vana aligned the nut with her claw and with just the smallest amount of pressure her claw pierced through the shell. Now that she had some leverage Vana was able to pull the rest apart with her hands.

Samuel on the other hand took a page from Mr Darcy's book. He placed two walnuts in his palm and using both hands he pressed them together. It took all his strength but eventually the shells shattered and he could get at the food.

"How did you do that?" Tamara asked knowing Samuel was not the most physically impressive person in the world. "No secret, I just practiced it until I could do it" Samuel answered.

Unsurprisingly the walnuts were both larger and far more delicious than any Samuel had ever had in his old life. What made this, all the, more incredible was that he had never been a big fan of nuts and he was wolfing them down.

Vana looked up at the sky and saw something she did not like "it's going to rain soon" she said. Vana had spent her old life one step away from starvation, alongside the knowledge of what was and was not edible she also become good as judge what the weather was going to be like a few hours from now.

Neither Samuel or Tamara questioned it, they had both learned that Vana knew what she was talking about and they had never heard her tell a lie. The hurriedly set up camp just a few metres from the stream and waited for the rain.

Vana thought she might have misjudged it but around forty-five minutes later it started to rain. They had arranged their tents so that they faced each other and the rain struck the sides. This way they could keep the entrances open and talk to one another. The three of them enjoyed shouting at each other, trying to be heard over the downpour.

There were two problems however the first was that they could not start a fire so it would be a cold tea today. The second was they had used up most of their supplied already so someone would have to go out in the rain and find something.

Samuel pulled on a rain poncho and stepped outside, despite the heavy rain Samuel remained dry. He stepped through the damp sand and stuck his head in the girl's tent, Tamara who was busy drawing said "if you've come here for anything untoward you can forget it you dirty bugger." Samuel chuckled and said "why would I want to spend my evening with an oily faced teenager." Tamara look at him and said "my skin isn't oily."

Vana and Samuel smiled and he said "Vana I'm going out to find something to eat." Vana replied "are you sure? I can go instead." "No I always liked the rain besides someone has to look after Tamara" Samuel said. Tamara ignored them. "You're certain?" asked Vana. "Oh, don't worry about, to be honest I feel sorry for you" Samuel answered. "Why?" Vana asked confused. "Because I'm leaving you alone with that" he said pointing at Tamara.

He turned and bolted from the tent. A split second later Tamara's hands grasped at where Samuel had been "I'll get you, monkey!" she screamed. "I'm an ape not a monkey!" Samuel shouted as he vanished into the scrub forest.

Samuel followed the stream, it was a so narrow you could jump over it but it gave him a way to find his way back. It would not be dark for several hours but it was easy to get turned around in an unfamiliar place and that coupled with the rain was just asking for trouble.

He just needed to find a fruit tree or something, the walnut tree was not available, they had already picked all the edible nuts. He saw some crayfish in the stream but he was not desperate enough to eat them raw. Samuel thought about the irony of fire, the more you needed it the harder it was to make.

Despite the apparent frustrating situation, Samuel was rather calm, the sound of the rain pattering against his hood was soothing, if the rain kept up he would have an extremely comfortable sleep. There was just something about hearing the rain outside, while you were warm and dry that made Samuel feel snug. He wriggled around in his poncho as he thought about it.

He spotted a large tree and sheltering underneath its branches were a couple of Moa. Samuel had to suppress a squeal and felt he could spend a few minutes with them. He stood beside the birds, they were not bothered, one gave Samuel a quick peak and after determining that he was neither edible or a threat they ignored him and focused on keeping dry.

He looked up at the sky and wondered. If they were alive perhaps their predator was, the Haast's eagle, a massive and powerful raptor capable of taking down even a creature the size of a Moa.

Five, ten, fifteen minute passed but eventually Samuel realised that he had people waiting for him and if he was too long they would start worrying. He left the birds and continued his search.

After another five minutes, he found some strawberry plants. This was a good find and Samuel stuffed his pockets with as many as he could carry. He had enough to keep the two of the them happy until morning but he wished he had brought a bag to he could carry a few more.

Keeping by the stream had been a good idea and it was easy to find his way back. The girls had closed the tent flap so Samuel knocked at best he could on leather and said "are you two decent in there?"

He heard some rummaging inside the tent and the front opened a fist came down on Samuel's head and he let out a yelp. It was not particularly painful it was more the shock that had caused him to shout. "What was that for?" Samuel shouted.

"It's your own fault, you took too long and I was starting to get worried" Tamara called out from the tent. "I found some Moa, alright?" Samuel explained. Tamara scoffed and said "you and those bloody birds." Samuel crawled into the tent pulling down his hood and replied "look you're not my mother or my wife so stop acting like it." Tamara smacked him on his head again, though it was far too light for it to be considered a hit and said "well someone has to or you would drown yourself just to see how deep the lake is and who said you could come in here?"

Samuel was getting a little annoyed and said "look if you keep this up I'll give you a hug." Tamara looked at his dripping wet poncho and shuddered at the thought of being frozen by it. "I didn't mean to make you worry, I'm sorry" Samuel said with a light smile. Tamara quiet for a bit but eventually she said "well so long as you're sorry" and she smiled back.

"I found these" Samuel said passing Vana a handful of the oversized fruit. It was tight fit inside the girl's tent, even if it was larger than his own, Samuel had just not designed it to hold more people. They chatted about the day and Vana decided to see just how much Samuel knew about his beloved birds.

Neither Vana or Tamara knew what they had let themselves in for and Samuel talked and talked, they were astounded that anyone could survive on so little breath. For almost an hour Samuel told them everything he knew about them he also mentioned the Haast's eagle which concerned them. He reassured them that even if it was around, it would not consider them prey.

They talked until sundown and Tamara was now ready for bed so the girls kicked Samuel out and he went back to his tent. He removed his Poncho and hung it up from a cord running along the length of his tent.

Samuel snuggled up beneath his blankets and focused on the rain hitting the tent wall, just as he expected he felt incredibly relaxed. He let all the thoughts of the day melt away and drifted off to sleep.

The next thing he knew the sun was hitting the side of his tent and steadily heating it up. He stayed inside as long as he could manage but in the end, it just became unbearable and Samuel clambered out of the tent.

He was once again the first one up, the sand was still moist from the night before, he might make some sandcastles.

He took his bowl, toothbrush and a flannel and went to the lake side. He cleaned his face and torso but as he brushed his teeth he felt something was wrong.

Looking up he spat out the water in his mouth and his toothbrush fell to the ground. There was an island sitting just a few dozen metres from the shore, it was big, covered in trees and it was certainly not there the day before.

Samuel was transfixed, his mind tried to come up with a logical reason as to how an island could spring up overnight but the only thing that could explain it was that a wizard did it. He did not budge for almost an hour, until Vana finally woke up and confused as to why a fire had not been started asked Samuel "what's going on?"

Her question was answered the moment she looked out at the water and she stood beside him and said "how the hell did we miss that?" Samuel replied "we didn't." Vana looked at him and said "what do you mean we didn't islands don't just pop out of the water." "Well this one did" Samuel replied. "How?" Vana asked. "No idea" Samuel answered.

They kept staring as if, if they looked away it would vanish. Samuel clenched his hand and realising that his toothbrush was gone he looked at the ground. It had not gone far but the bristles were covered in sand so he rinsed them off in the lake and finished brushing his teeth. This simple act made him feel grounded at least this still made sense.

The island was not large compared to others but it would easily hold fifty people. At this distance, it was hard to tell but he supposed it was about twenty to thirty metres long. It had a collection plants ranging from oaks to small bushes and there were birds and even squirrels living among the trees.

As the day got warmer Tamara started to stir and she stuck her head out of her tent. "What the heck it that!?" Tamara shouted. Vana and Samuel turned around to explain what was going on.

When Samuel opened his mouth, Tamara opened with her eyes, even from this distance Samuel could see they were filled with awe. She raised her hand and pointed behind them. Samuel could hear, the sound of, water being breached by a huge object, the last time he had heard that sound was when he had seen a blue whale come to the surface for a breath.

Samuel turned around and saw a head rise out of the water and Samuel shouted "it's a turtle! It's one hell of a turtle!" Water rolled of the side of its head, the huge creature opened its nostrils and a spout of water was blown from them, just like a whale. The birds on its back were wholly undisturbed and continued to sing to one another. The water jet was carried by the breeze, turned into a fine mist, and fell on Vana and Samuel "Lovely" Vana said.

"It's a turtle, the size of a whale, with trees growing on its back" said Samuel. "Was there something funky in those berries we ate last night?" he asked Vana. Tamara finally dared to get closer and she said "impossible I didn't eat any and I can see it too."

Despite the attention that the three of them were giving the island turtle, the animal itself couldn't care less. It took in a huge lungful of air, so huge that it took thirty second before it was done and then lowered its head back below the water. The water it displaced briefly pushed to shore over Samuel's feet and after that it was impossible to tell it was a turtle at all. "It has trees growing on its back" Samuel mumbled.

A few minutes of staring at the motionless shell and finally the spell the creature had on them was broken. The three of them returned to their camp in silence and sat down in the sand. "I don't suppose you've seen anything like that before?" Samuel asked Vana who was the best travelled out of all of them. She shook her head and said "no I have never seen one of those before" then an idea cropped up in her head "say do you think that was the island we saw in the distance a few days ago?"

Tamara and Samuel thought about it and concluded that it was probably the case "well at least you don' have to worry about adding it to your map" Samuel said.

None of them wanted to leave the island turtle, it was the most incredible thing any of them had seen in their lives and the girls began to understand how the Moa could captivate Samuel so completely.

If anyone had told Samuel that such a creature existed he would have dismissed it as fanciful storytelling and yet there it was and true to his nature Samuel went to his tent, took out a quill and a sheet of paper, at the very top he wrote "Island Turtle" he then paused and thought about how it looked and then beside he wrote "Chelonia Insula."

With the full force of his passion Samuel jotted down every detail he could gleam from the immobile colossus, Tamara immediately started to draw and Vana assisted both of them in any way she could.

It was hard to say what could have possibly evolved into such a leviathan but judging from simple appearance it most closely resembled a gigantic green sea turtle, though Samuel knew that it was foolish to group animals together based on physical traits but he had nothing else to go on.

Tamara was focusing as hard as she could to create the best picture possible. She captured the turtle mid-rise, the water still falling from it and birds flying between the trees. Twenty minutes later the turtle lifted its head again, took another breathe but there was something different about it. The turtles mouth was full of green weeds and lake grasses, that was why it came to the shore, it was to that it could eat.

The sound of the turtle swallowing was audible from where they were sitting and Samuel watched the bulge in its throat move downwards like a wave. The turtle put its head down but rested both its eyes and nostrils above the water line. Using its huge flippers, it swam several metres and glided to a stop, its head dipped below the surface once more and they assumed it had started to eat again.

"It must eat a lot" Tamara said. Samuel nodded but his mind began to think about those trees on its back. They were big, judging from the size it must have been growing there for almost a century. Samuel pointed it out to the other two and Vana said "it must be an old fellow then."

That was interesting but it was not what he had meant. If that tree was there it meant that the turtle must not dive, if it did the tree would split because of the force of water. So, the question was why would the turtle not dive, the answer Samuel believed was it must want to keep the plants on its back alive.

"I think it has a symbiotic relationship with those trees" Samuel explained. "What's that mean?" asked Vana. "Well a thing that size needs a lot of food, and plants convert sunlight and carbon dioxide in their food, right?" Samuel said. "I suppose so" Tamara replied. "So, I think the turtle gives the plants a safe place to grow and a constant water and nutrient supply the trees might give the turtle some of the food them make" Samuel explained. "How?" asked Tamara. Samuel shrugged his shoulders and said "no idea."

The turtle spent several hours hoovering up every scrap of green it found, leaving a bare road of silt behind it. The three of them would have loved to have spent the entire day just following it but it was Samuel, of all people, who decided that they needed to get going. They packed up their camp and left the huge animal behind.

Chapter 6

Even after several days the turtle made up most of their conversations Samuel, in particular, had much fun speculating about how something that astounding functioned and how it came to be.

In between a talk on how much something that size would need to eat Samuel had a thought. "Girls how long have we been traveling?" he asked. Vana replied "fourteen days." The expedition stopped and all three of them sat down in the sand. They had been out here for half their allotted time they would have to decide whether to keep going or turn back.

"It doesn't look like we are anywhere near the end" Tamara said looking out into the distance. "Yep it's one big lake" Samuel added. "Thank you for stating the obvious" Tamara said. "Any time sweetie" Samuel replied.

"We do have about sixteen days and we could probably get away with one or two extra" Vana offered. Tamara and

Samuel nodded, if they were a couple of days late it might cause some worry but it would certainly not cause the panic that a week's delay would. "But even so should we risk it?" Samuel asked waving over the water "I mean it could take us another month to walk around that."

Samuel eye caught something and said "I think there's another island turtle out there" pointing to a speck on the horizon. Vana and Tamara looked and Vana said "oh yeah, I wonder how many are out there." "A pity we can't ride one of them" Tamara said and the three of them laughed.

"I say we leave it to a vote" Samuel offered. Tamara and Vana thought about it and then nodded in agreement "ok I'll go first" Samuel said "I say we go back." "Really?" Tamara asked "you're the one who arranged this whole thing." "I know but I don't want to make your mom worry" Samuel explained.

It was Vana's turn next and she said "I say we keep going." "One each" Samuel said "ok Tamara you have the deciding vote." The two of them looked at her and waited for her decision, it was a difficult decision for Tamara, she desperately wanted to see what was further along but she also agreed with Samuel it would be wrong to make her mom worry like that.

Tamara ummed and ahhed, she sighed and snorted while Samuel and Vana sat patiently for her to answer. As the minutes turned into an hour Tamara who was currently chewing her own hair finally made her decision and said "we keep going."

"Well the people have spoken" Samuel said and stood up. "There's only three of us" Vana said. "It's a figure of speech" Samuel explained. They continued on their way and Samuel reminded them "we still have about two days to change your minds so you can keep thinking about it."

Though Samuel would go along with them he could not shake the feeling that they were doing the wrong thing not that it would lead to a death or anything just that it was wrong.

The next day passed without incident and neither Tamara nor Vana changed their choices. "oh well we're committed now" Samuel thought on the sixteenth day. Up ahead there was a sub adult Moa looking for gizzard stones in the sand "that should cheer me up" Samuel whispered.

A shadow appeared over the Moa and the next thing any of them knew the huge bird had been pushed to the ground and a massive eagle was perched on its hind quarters with one claw lodged in the pelvis and the other on the skull. The moa had been dead before it hit the ground.

"Shit!" Samuel shouted and put his arms out to stop the others from getting closer. The bird's appearance startled everyone, "Haast's Eagle?" Tamara asked. "Haast's Eagle" Samuel answered. Vana extended her claws just to be on the safe side.

Despite the obvious power of the Eagle had it was clearly nervous about the three of them. It started at them with it piercing golden eyes, determining if they were a threat. Samuel could not tell if it was unfamiliar with people or if it was and knew that they could chase it from its kill.

As Samuel's heartbeat slowed he took a better look at the animal. For all its ferocity, it was a gorgeous creature, it must have had a three-metre wingspan with a beautiful tail, it look as though it was half a metre long and if Samuel remembered correctly that would make it a she. The Eagle stood as tall as a six-year-old child and was covered in mahogany feathers.

The Eagle must have felt if they were going to do anything it would have happened by now and started to tear into the Moa's body with its beak. Samuel was impressed at how strong and sharp her beak was, it functioned just like a meat hook digging into the flesh and then ripping it apart.

"We should keep moving" Tamara said. The three of them went around the bird who stopped once to see what they were doing and then went straight back to it meal. The Haast's Eagle had ripped out dozens of feathers which were now lying on the sand. Samuel collected a couple and placed them in his writing bag, though they were so long it was a tight fit, so he could study them later.

As he looked at the eagles back he noticed that one of her flight feathers had fallen out during the attack and was now sticking out of the sand just like Excalibur. "I have to have that" Samuel mumbled and edges closer to the bird.

"Samuel what are you doing? Don't tell me you plan on training that thing" Tamara said imagining the worst possible scenario. He had not even considered that but he turned around and gave Tamara a smile that clearly said "thanks for the idea." "Oh no, you get back here right now!" Tamara ordered. Samuel told her "I'm trying to get that feather." "It's right underneath it, that thing will rip your face off" Vana said trying to dissuade him but Samuel was in obsessive naturalist mode and he replied "that thing is a she."

The eagle must have been starving because he got within two metres until she finally noticed what was happening behind her. She glowered at Samuel her pupil dilated to allowing more light. Samuel, crouched in the sand took another step forward, the eagle flapped her wings and hunkered down ready to defend her kill.

He inched closer and she tensed up. Samuel was in striking distance now, he had one shot, if he missed he would learn what it was like to get stabbed by those talons.

Samuel went for it, his hand clasped the feather and he immediately ran away. The eagle pounced her talons narrowly missing the back of his head. As she watched Samuel run away the eagle jumped forwards a couple to time to hammer home the point and then returned to her food. He felt, pretty, good about himself and gently placed the eagles feather alongside the Moa's. Then two hands slapped him round the back of the head "one of these days that attitude going to get you killed!" Tamara shouted. "That hurt" Samuel moaned. "Good" Vana replied.

Once the pain in the back of his head had died down he took the time to inspect the feather he had risked his life to collect. In many ways, it was unremarkable, just like any other feather a person had ever found on a beach but to Samuel who had spent years studying birds it told him much.

It was about a foot long but Samuel felt that was a little short for an animal that size but he realised that due to the size of the eagles prey it needed to focus on strength not endurance, it also allowed the eagle to dart through the trees to strike without warning.

Tamara watched as Samuel rotated the feather in his fingers and asked "are you sure that one of those things won't attack us?" Samuel looked at her and said "No I wouldn't think so." Tamara squinted and said "you saw how it took down that moa, what could one of those things do to us?" Samuel smiled and told her "exactly we're just too small to bother with."

She was not entirely satisfied but she was willing go on a bit of faith and let it lie. Changing the subject Samuel asked Vana "So how is your flower pressing coming along." Vana knew what he was trying to do but she really wanted to tell someone about it "good I've got thirty-five different types now" she said.

Vana enjoyed talking about her new hobby and Samuel had just as much fun listening to her, asking her questions about how and where she found each flower. "Hey love birds are we gonna set up camp or what?" Tamara interrupted their conversation and pointed at the sun. To both Samuel and Vana's amazement they had been talking for hours and Samuel said "sorry Tamara we completely left you out." Tamara waved her hand dismissively and said "I don't mind, too be honest I enjoyed having some time to think."

During the remaining hour, Samuel wrote a section about the Haast's eagle, Tamara drew a picture and Vana went out hunting for supper and flowers. Vana came back with a couple of rabbits and Samuel cooked up a stew.

The evening passed at a snail's pace after dinner, which was a welcome relief, they spent the remaining light doing nothing much at all. Vana was examining her flowers, Tamara was playing with her tunic and Samuel had a lot of fun cloud watching.

Tamara and Vana went to bed but Samuel decided to stay up for a while and look at the stars. As he looked at the twinkling lights he was remined of his cavern and rather surprisingly he felt homesick. He had felt this feeling many times but it was truly astounding that he wanted to return to his cave and not his family. Then a voice in his head said "how dare you not want to see your mom and dad again."

Samuel shook his head and moaned "not this again." The voice was wrong he did want to see his parents and tell them what had happened and all he had seen but at the same time he did not want to leave his friends behind. Samuel rubbed his finger and said "Not that it matters, I don't even know where here is let alone home." He looked up at the stars again and thought that maybe if he had bothered to learn astronomy he might be able to read the stars better, he could make out Orion but that meant little.

"Well shoulda, woulda, coulda" Samuel said and went to bed, he hoped he would have no nightmares tonight.

Unfortunately, Samuel did but to his relief when he woke up he could no longer remember it, it had something do to with darkness but the rest was a total blur. He mentioned it to Vana and Tamara, they were concerned, nightmares were not fun but they could not actually hurt you. Samuel nodded in agreement and three of them set off.

Two more days passed and nothing of real note happened, they did see a third island turtle in the distance and though the rest of them missed it Tamara swore she saw a Haast's eagle swooping down on something in the distance.

On the next day, however while Samuel was at the top of a peach tree, gathering lunch; an unusual thing in of itself, for the top branches to support his weight, though not unheard of. He spotted something unnatural on the horizon, it looked artificial. Samuel wondered what it could be and then it hit him, it was a village.

"Girls I think there a village over there" he shouted down from the tree tops. "What? You mean like ours?" Tamara called. "No I mean one made from dreams and kitten whiskers" Samuel replied sarcastically. "Hold on I'm coming up" Tamara said. She pressed herself up against the tree's trunk coiled around it and began to climb using her entire tail as one massive foot.

A few seconds later Tamara's head popped out of the leaves and she looked at where Samuel was pointing. "Yep those do look like buildings" Tamara agreed as Samuel pulled twigs and leaves from her hair. "We should go down and discuss it with Vana" Tamara said and Samuel replied "right." As Tamara began to climb down he had an odd thought and mumbled "if this were a book, we'd fall out of the tree now."

Neither of them fell out of the tree though Samuel did prick his finger on a sharp branch "typical" Samuel moaned as he sucked his little finger.

"Well what did it look like?" Vana asked when Samuel finally got down. "It does look like a village or at least there are buildings over there. "How far?" She asked. "I would say about three miles" then Samuel remembered they those two had no concept of a mile and added "a shortish walk, wouldn't take us all day to get there and back, even if we spent most of our day there."

"We're going?" Vana asked puzzled. "Of course, we could do with some food and you two deserve a roof over your head" Samuel answered "Tamara I need you to turn the cuteness up to eleven" he added grasping one of her shoulder. "I'm not some performing animal, it takes time and preparation to be as adorable as this" she replied gesturing to herself. "You'll have to make do" Samuel said grabbing both her and Vana by the wrist and pulling them behind him.

"Samuel, I'm not sure that this is a good idea, I mean what if they see me? what if they see you?" Vana said. "As long as Tamara's there to vouch for you, you'll be fine" Samuel reassured her. "I not so sure about that" Vana replied.

"I just realised that I didn't see any fields around the buildings" Tamara said. "Yeah now that you mention it" Samuel said "maybe they have orchards rather than crop fields" he offered. "Does that mean they have cider?" Vana asked. Samuel and Tamara chuckled and he replied "yeah probably."

As they got closer all three of them could tell something was wrong. They must have been no further than one hundred metres away and they could hear nothing. At the forest village, you could clearly hear the villagers shouting over one another but here there was only the sound of bird song.

Unlike home there was no clear divide between where the scrubland ended and the village began. The three of them waited on what they assumed was the border and watched. The only movement any of them saw was a rat that darted between two of the buildings.

"Wait here" Samuel instructed as he tentatively edged forwards. "No, we all go together!" Tamara shouted in a whisper. Samuel looked her in the eye and said "look I've got a theory but I have to make certain that I'm right." "Then just tell us" Vana said. "I can't, if I'm wrong then it will be better if only one of us goes" Samuel explained. "That still doesn't make much sense, it just sounds like you're being melodramatic" Tamara replied. "I am a bit but please just trust me" Samuel explained.

The girls agreed but told him that if they heard so much as a mild whine then they would come barrelling in. Samuel pressed himself up against one of the buildings walls and then peered around the corner. Nothing just like he expected.

Samuel walked down one of the streets that was now overgrown with grass with several trees taking root. He opened the door of the nearest house and went inside, Samuel could smell mildew and rot, inside one of the rooms he found that it was missing small Knick-knacks but the large furniture was still here.

He checked four more houses and found the exact same pattern and then returned to Tamara and Vana. "Well what's going on?" Vana asked. "The entire place it abandoned" Samuel answered.

"This is creepy" Tamara said walking down what would have been the market place. Tamara entire life experience had told her that villages should be filled with people and the fact that the village was laid out almost exactly like hers only intensified the feeling.

"What happened? Why would everyone just leaved?" Vana asked greatly confused. Even though it was not obvious Samuel knew that the question was directed at him "well if I were a betting man I would say the same thing that had almost dislodged you lot" he replied. Tamara realised what he meant and said "you mean the fields dried up?" Samuel nodded.

"It's sad more than anything else" Vana said and Samuel nodded how many memories these people must have had here and they had to leave or starve.

As the three of them explored the abandoned village Samuel went into what was once a field and found that there were still a few crops that had not yet been pushed out by the native plants. They were small and nowhere near as impressive as the ones back home "I hope that my crops aren't not too badly damaged when I got back" he said to himself.

"Told you we would get some supplies" he said dangling the vegetables in Vana's face. "Looking at them I'm starting to wish you hadn't" she replied looking displeased. Samuel sighed and said "you know the food in that place has really spoiled you, where I'm from you would be ecstatic to find these."

Samuel cooked them a savoury dinner and they continued exploring. They found the town hall, much the same as the one back home except this one had stone floors rather than wooden ones, back home the planks were there so that the cold stone did not sap out the Lamia's heat. As soon as Tamara touched the stone floor she let out a squeal that echoed throughout the building. "You know for all your tough girl act you sure are a wuss" Samuel said. "Shut up" Tamara replied.

"It's bigger than the one back home" Tamara said from the door. "Must be more people lived here" Vana said. Arranged in the hall were hundreds of chairs, still left were the villagers had sat during these peoples last meeting, like a moment frozen in time. "Just think what would have happened if you hadn't dropped into our lives this would have happened to us" Tamara added. "Yeah well if you hadn't given me a chance it wouldn't have mattered" Samuel replied with a smile and Tamara smiled back.

"There's no door back there" Vana pointed out on the opposite side of the room. "Oh, yeah that was Samuel's idea" Tamara said recalling the fire and that several people had become trapped in the village hall. "See it's not just you that takes all the credit" Samuel said patting Vana on the shoulder.

They left the hall and found the house that had survived the elements best and placed their things inside the living room, after they made sure that the building would not fall on their heads. They laid out their mattresses and lit the fireplace. "Are you sure that we should be sleeping here?" Tamara asked. "Why? you afraid that ghosts will come and get you?" Samuel said making wooing noises. "Shut up" Tamara replied.

"Been years since I had a roof over my head and it feels like decades" Samuel said. "You live in a cave with central heating and indoor plumbing" Tamara stated. "You know what I mean" Samuel said "wait how do you know what plumbing and central heating are?" he added puzzled. "You told me about them, remember?" Tamara replied. "Did I?" Samuel replied unable to recall that specific event.

"Why are we setting up camp anyway? It's still light out" Vana asked. "Saves time later" Tamara explained "though I would have preferred somewhere that doesn't look exactly like my living room" she added. "All right we'll go spend the entire day in the village hall" Samuel said with a smile. "Creepy, rundown copy of my house is fine" Tamara said.

When it was finished, Samuel said he was going to walk around see what he could find. "Not without me you're not" Tamara said and got of her mattress. "And you two aren't leaving me alone" Vana added. "What are you afraid of? You fought a human remember" Samuel said bringing up how the two of them met. "I'm not afraid it's just boring when you're alone" Vana answered, rather unconvincingly.

This time they explored the outer regions of the village, focusing mainly on the fields and the scrub forest beyond. "Hey if their field all went barren then how come there's stuff growing in it now?" Tamara asked. "Well I would first of all, like to point out that it's just a theory and second how long would you say this place has been abandoned?" Samuel replied. "Judging by the damage I'd say five to ten years" Vana answered. "Well if you leave it alone and give it time land will rejuvenate itself" Samuel explained.

Samuel noticed something shiny sticking out of the earth and he pulled it free. He wiped it clean and was astounded by what he saw, it was a coin, he had no idea who was on it and he could not read the language but it was unmistakably a coin, it was money.

"What's that?" Vana said leaning over his shoulder. "Do you remember what I told you about how humans traded things?" "Yes" Vana replied. Samuel handed the silver disk to her and said "well that right there is a coin."

Both Tamara and Vana both studied the coin, Samuel had often explained the alien concept of currency but even with it right in front of their eyes neither of them could understand how this was worth food or anything for that matter. "Do you think it was made by the villagers?" Tamara asked. Samuel scratched his head and replied "it's possible but if they were anything like you then it would have just been a pretty piece of metal." He took the coin from them and remembered that there were two sides "I have been here a while" Samuel said as he flipped it over. He wiped the rest of the grime of to reveal a series of swirls, it took him only an instant to realise what it was, the double helix of D.N.A.

Samuel was certain now that the villagers had not made this none of them had the technology to see a cell let alone the two nanometres of a strand of D.N.A. This was made by human hands.

Unfortunately, this was very little to go on, if only it had been a euro, a yen, a pound anything he was familiar with, but this, as far as he was concerned it might as well be written in hieroglyphics. Samuel explained his theory to the girls and Tamara asked "so how did it get here?" he shrugged his shoulders and said "not that complicated, someone lost it and then it was found again probably kept as a trinket and was lost once again when everybody left."

He handed the coin back and Tamara and Vana gawked at it while Samuel kept looking. He found more things the people had left behind, nails, belt buckles, old rags. Samuel picked up everything he found feeling that he should keep some record of the people who lived here, he was certain that in a thousand years it would make some historian very happy.

"Tamara, could you make a few sketches of the buildings? I'm sure your friends back home would like to see them" Samuel suggested. "Good idea" Tamara said "I'll do it when we get back."

Vana went wandering around a corner and then called to them "found their barn." Tamara and Samuel followed and began looking around, though Vana said that she did not like the look of the barn itself and they should not enter. "Yeah, that hasn't held up well" Tamara said.

They found signs of the same animals that they kept at the village pigs, chickens, sheep, cows, ostriches, goats, kangaroos, geese, and ducks. Though there was one pen that Tamara could not explain it had a large pool of water in the middle. "For the geese and ducks maybe" Vana suggested. "A little big" Tamara replied. "Maybe they had a lot of them" Vana added.

"Where's Samuel?" Vana asked when she looked over her shoulder. "Oh, that bloody man" Tamara said rubbing her forehead. "Samuel!" Vana shouted but she got no reply. "Let's see I were Samuel where would I run off to" Tamara said rubbing her chin. "Well you probably would have seen a new animal and run after it like a mad man" Vana added. Tamara sighed and said "let's go look for him."

The pair of them covered over three quarter of the village but could not find a trace, they were starting to get worried. Vana then heard a noise from one of the old houses and they went inside. They found Samuel in the corner of the old kitchen holding a large goanna. "Well I hit the nail on the head" Vana said cheerfully. Tamara breathed a sigh of relief and then smacked him.

"Stop hitting me!" Samuel shouted. "Then stop doing stupid things!" Tamara shouted back. "What it's just a goanna, it's not like it can kill me" Samuel explained. Tamara sighed again and explained "why didn't you tell us what you were doing?" "Because if I had stopped to tell you I would have lost it" he replied showing them the lizard he caught. "You're like a child" Tamara complained. "That's what makes me so loveable" Samuel explained.

The goanna struggled in Samuel's grip and he stroked its head and said "don't worry I'm not going to hurt you." Tamara and Vana let their annoyance go, the accepted that this behaviour was just par for the course with Samuel, though they wouldn't stop hitting him when he did something stupid.

After Samuel, had examined the animal he let it go and the goanna scurried off. The sun was going down and they headed back to camp. Tamara started drawing the buildings and as an additional punishment for Samuel she told him that she would not be drawing that lizard for the next couple of days.

Chapter 7

When morning came the three of them were anxious to leave, they had already used up a lot of time and they still had no idea how far away home was. They did however get a pleasant surprise; a family of Moa were making their way through the village and following a large male were a dozen chicks.

They were large for a baby bird, covered in brown speckled feathers and the way they walked was almost as if they were jumping with joy. "I'll definitely be drawing them" Tamara said preemptible answering Samuel's question.

The chicks must have been born recently as they had no fear, they walked up to the three of them, daddy watching carefully, and started pecking at them. Vana took some left-over fruit from this morning's breakfast and offered it to the nearest bird. The tiny animal inspected it and then gave it an experimental bite. All three of them sighed at the adorable display.

Daddy clearly felt that this was enough playing with the odd featherless birds, he started to walk away and let out a low call. The chicks responded almost immediately and started to follow their father.

Reinvigorated by the unexpected guests the trio made good time, they emerged from the scrubland and back onto the beach about a quarter of a mile from where they had entered. Samuel stopped briefly to refill the water canteens and then they continued.

"I wonder what everyone is doing back home" Vana said. "Oh, the usual I suppose, minor problems being fixed, mom, Mrs Odalinde and Mr Handus being driven up the wall. "You know I'm starting to feel a little bad about leaving" Vana told them. There was silence for a few moments and then Tamara said "yeah I feel like that to, I do hope my mom isn't having too much trouble." Vana smiled and said "I sure their all fine after all life is pretty sedate back there." The two of them laughed at how silly they had been though deep down they could still feel just the slightest hint of guilt.

Samuel of course had no such worries, he was perfectly aware that the villagers would be positively ecstatic knowing he was gone. In fact, he was fairly sure that the second Pancha had returned home and told them the evil human was gone all the children started playing in the forest singing the monsters gone. "Little buggers" Samuel thought.

Before the sunset, the landscape abruptly changed once again. The scrubland gave way to a series of shallow, slow moving rivers. There were islands of sand covered with grasses and trees. It looked like a mangrove swamp but Samuel knew this should not be possible as mangroves only occurred along the coast.

"How the heck I'm I supposed to get across that?" Tamara complained as she put up her tent. That was a good question, this was not a simple matter of building a raft, the network of waters ways was so tangled that they could easily get lost if they tried to navigate it. They could not sail around it, it stretched on for miles and it would take weeks to build something that could handle that kind of journey.

"Let's think about and we'll try and come up with a solution tomorrow" Samuel said rubbing his eyes, he was starting to think that this trip was a bad idea.

Everyone was silent around that campfire, Samuel could not be bothered to cook so he made a fruit salad instead. Samuel tried his best to come up with a solution but he kept drawing up blanks, if only he had said sixty days then none of this would be a problem.

He was beginning to think that the only way was to just barrel on through. The beach though much narrower and disconnected in the mangroves, was still there so they should be able to navigate it easily. Even so the three big problems still presented themselves one was keeping their stuff, especially the paper, dry. Two was finding a place to sleep every night that would not flood and finally making sure Tamara stayed warm.

Logic told him that the second problem should not exist after all. Mangroves that existed by a lake shouldn't have big tides however he had learned not to underestimate how ridiculous thing could get here.

Perhaps Tamara would not have as much trouble as he supposed while it was true that she hated the cold it was not as if immersing herself in cold water would knock her out instantly, if they timed it right they might be able to island hop.

He was tired now her would bring it up with them tomorrow for now he would sleep.

Unsurprisingly Tamara was not thrilled at the prospect of slogging through cold water. "Then please come up with a better idea" Samuel said. Tamara sat down, coiled her tail around her body, so that all was visible was a few strands of hair poking out of the gaps and started moaning.

"Are you sure she can do it?" Vana asked. Samuel looked at Vana and explained "It won't be pleasant but Tamara actually an excellent swimmer" Samuel paused for a moment and then, feeling is inner biologist rise to the surface, added "The problem is that Tamara's too smart, you see most cold blooded animals are good swimmers, it's just Tamara can remember vividly how unpleasant it is to be cold, it's all up here" Samuel tapped his head to clarify what he meant.

Samuel decided to get the ball rolling he removed his boot, socks, armour and rolled up his trousers, Vana stayed behind and tried to coax Tamara out of her coil. He held the supplies safety above the water line. It was unpleasant at first and he felt a brief pang of sympathy for Tamara, then his blood vessel constricted, his skin became the same temperature as the water around him and it became rather enjoyable. Yet when the water came up to his chest he did feel rather foolish for rolling up his trouser legs.

Tamara was out though still unhappy, Samuel offered his hand and Tamara took it, holding onto his hand filled Tamara with a comfort that she normally felt when with her mother; something she had noticed happening a few years ago.

Tamara slid in the water and she winced. Vana brought up the rear making sure she was on hand if anything went wrong. While Samuel and Vana walked, Tamara swam, her long tail gracefully undulating from side to side. "You miserable bastard, I swear one day I'll strike back at you like a viper!" she shouted through gasping breaths.

Helping her onto the sand bank, Tamara spread herself out on the warm sand, the grains sticking to her damp clothes. They would wait until Tamara was feeling better before they tried again "I'm proud of you" Samuel said patting Tamara on her head. "Whatever" Tamara replied.

Samuel let her rest and spent a few moments inspecting the mangroves, he stuck his finger in the stream and sucked it. Not a trace of salt, he supposed that this made it a swamp but it looked nothing like any he had seen before, if Samuel suspicion were correct that would mean that this place was artificial as well.

It was no small feat to plant entire forests or create unnatural mangroves, he wondered how technological advanced these people must have been. A part of him thought that instead of technology it was magic but he had seen nothing to suppose that it existed, Tamara, Vana and even the Islands turtles could all be explained by science.

Vana had not been idle, she had already moved all the supplied to the next sand bank and was preparing Tamara for the next run. It was further this time, at least twenty metres and they wanted to be certain that Tamara could handle it.

Just like before Samuel held her hands and led her into the water, Tamara cursed and started to swim. It took longer and drained Tamara considerably more this time, to help speed things up Samuel took out a towel and dried her tail. "Mmm, that feels good" Tamara said lying on her stomach. "Well don't get used to it or we'll soak all our towels" Samuel replied.

It was slow going, even slower than that time when Samuel had insisted on documenting every beetle he saw. By sunset they could still see the scrublands but no one was frustrated actual they were in high spirits, this was a difficult situation and they were besting it.

They stopped on a particularly large island and lit a fire but Samuel was not confident in sleeping on the ground so he suggested that they use the tents and rope to set up hammocks in the tree tops. As she had had the hardest time today Tamara had the final say.

The chance to sleep hanging from branches excited Tamara so she readily agreed. It took a little longer than usual to set up camp, they hung their things from the branches as well so that nothing could root around inside without their knowledge.

However, before they could get to bed they had to change out of their wet and sandy clothes. Samuel took a fresh top and some trousers and disappeared behind a tree. "You better not peep through the roots!" Tamara called as he vanished from sight. "Don't flatter yourself sweetie" Samuel shouted back.

Dangling four metres in the air, Samuel found himself surprisingly at ease, he had never been entirely confident with heights but that had been gradually improving over time. Samuel reached out to a nearby branch and then pulled hard and released. As Samuel's makeshift hammock began to rock gently, he sighed and settled down. He took the coin from his pocket and using the last of the light he read the writing around the edge "CREP SUBBER FRET EST", "meaningless" Samuel mumbled.

"Vana" Samuel called. "Yeah" she replied. "We haven't left anything on the ground, have we?" he asked. "I don't think so" she answered. "Well I guess we'll find out tomorrow" he said closing his eyes.

Samuel woke up feeling refreshed, so much so that he felt he could leap out of bed. He was about to so that but then he remembered that he was suspended over a large drop and stopped himself before his head was cracked open.

With great care Samuel clambered down the tree, he made an extra effort not to injure his naked feet not any of the exposed, and rather sharp, branches and landed straight into a river. Samuel's hunch had been right, the river had risen and the island that had once been dry was now covered in a few centimetres of water he sighed and said "I hate being right all the time."

Annoyed that he would not have any warm breakfasts for a while Samuel sucked it up, opened his bag hanging from the tree and took out a pear. Sitting nestled between the tangled tree roots Samuel watched the water flow past and spotted a few fish through the crystal-clear water.

Taking another bite from his breakfast Samuel tried to remember what they were, they were long and thin, with an elongated skull filled with sharp teeth. It might have been fearsome if they were larger and not covered with those delightful brown spots. Then Samuel remembered it was a spotted gar, once again this made no sense as spotted gars lived in salt water, "sod it" Samuel mumbled, it was far too early in the morning to complain.

Vana, wakened by Samuel moaning said, annoyed that she had been brought out of a good dream "what's the matter?" "Just look down and you'll see" Samuel replied. It took Vana a while to coax herself from her blanket but in the end, she found the will to peer over the side of her hammock and said "Tamara's not going to like this."

She started to clamber out of bed and sat beside Samuel "this is actually rather comfortable" she said surprised. Samuel nodded in agreement and Vana said "I thought tide only occurred near the ocean." "Well it does occur near any body of water but most of the time it's barely noticeable" Samuel explained. "It'll go back, right?" she asked. Samuel handed her a pear and said "it better, Tamara's annoyed enough with me as it is."

To Samuel's relief the water did start to recede and as it went dozens of fiddler crabs emerged from the silt to feed on the small particles of food that the water had left behind and when their stomachs were full the males jousted with one another.

Tamara awoke later, she had slept well and she clambered down out of her hammock onto the sand. Samuel packed away her hammock for her and now that the water was gone they removed the bags from the branches.

The crabs were a little startled by the golden snake that had dropped in front of them. A particularly brave one walked up to her and gently pinched her tail. Tamara however did not react, the scales on her back were far too tough.

While they waited for Tamara to warm up Samuel took out a sheet of paper and made a few notes about the fiddler crabs and Vana climbed the trees looking for blossoms to add to her collection.

"Hey there are crabs here" Tamara called out sleepily. "Yeah it only took you half the morning to notice" Samuel replied. Unusually Tamara did not bite back, she just watched the animal wave its claws up and down in a futile attempt to scare her off. She just smiled and said "I like crabs."

The day wore on and the water level lowered even further, low enough that they could start ferrying their supplied to the next island. Tamara was now wide awake and she was not enjoying the prospect of another day of swimming through cold water.

Yet there was no other way and Samuel led her into the water and Tamara immediately started swearing again. In any other circumstance Samuel would be telling her to watch her language but considering what she was going through he felt it would be unfair to chastise her.

"There's got to be a better way" Tamara moaned as she warmed herself on the new patch of land. Vana rung the water from her tunic and looked up hoping that the inspiration would fall from the sky. A branch fell of one of the trees and into the water and an idea hit her "thank you tree" Vana said.

"Hey Tamara do you think you could move from branch to branch?" Vana asked pointing to the trees overhead. Tamara stared at the twigs and leaves and judged the distance, there was a sizeable gap between each tree line and the boughs that were strong enough to support her made that distance even wider. However, Tamara was very long over six meters and by the time she was eighteen she could be up to nine meters in length and to top it all off, she was like all Lamia's an excellent climber.

"Yeah I think I can make that" Tamara answered. Once she had warmed up again Tamara picked a suitable tree and began to climb. Both Samuel and Vana were stationed in the river below ready to respond in case anything went amiss.

Tamara pushed away the leaves and twigs until she could clearly see her destination, a particularly sturdy branch on the opposite bank. Slowly Tamara extended herself her tail uncoiling from the trees trunk like a fishing line. It was easy at first but as she reached that half way point her stomach muscles began to strain.

She was just a meter from her goal but she was now supported by only the base of her tail, she would have to rest soon, Tamara was strong but she tired quickly. Her strength faltered briefly and she almost fell.

Now positioned under the branch Tamara used up all her remaining strength and propelled herself upwards, he grabbed the bough with her hands and pulled herself up.

With her bulk now supported, it was easy to reel in the rest of herself in and she clambered down the tree head first and rested beside its trunk.

Vana and Samuel trudged out from the water and Samuel asked "How was it?" Tamara smiled and said "to be honest I doubt it's any easier than swimming." "Are you ever happy?" Samuel asked. "Only when your mouth is closed" Tamara replied with a cheeky smile.

It may have taken more physical effort on her part but it was undoubtedly faster than the old method. The next river was narrower than the last and was easier on Tamara who crossed it in a fraction of the time. The next one however was even wider than the first one and it was impossible for her to cross it from above.

This set up the pattern for the next few days, Tamara would hope that the next river was narrow enough to cross and swear at Samuel if it was not. On the fourth day, the three of them decided that they would take it easy, they would cross one or two rivers at most and just take the time to recharge. Samuel also used this time to wash his clothes and get rid of the sand that had wormed its way between every fibre.

While he was scrubbing, he noticed a black shape come towards him. Samuel mind raced at what it could be, he knew that crocodiles and sharks sometimes lived in mangroves and though none of the them had seen any so far did not mean they were not here. So, he immediately ran up the beach putting as much land as he could between them.

The shadow got closer until a turtle crawled its way onto the beach, it was a big thing almost as large as Samuel was. Samuel laughed at himself and moved closer. The turtle was curious about Samuel but not afraid. Samuel placed his hand on its head, the turtle sniffed him.

Samuel tried to pinpoint what species it was, it looked like a green sea turtle except it was far too large and it had pits in its shell, that were unlike anything he had seen before. "Hey girls come look at this" Samuel called. Vana and Tamara dropped what they were doing and walked down the beach.

"Wow" Tamara said as she kneeled beside it "can it touch it?" she asked. "Yeah just be gentle" Samuel answered. Tamara and Vana began to stroke the turtle who did not seem bothered "his shells weird, its smooth but it's also full of cracks" Vana said. "It looks like one of the island turtles just smaller and without the trees on its back" Tamara said. "Maybe it's a baby" Vana suggested.

"You are a genius" Samuel said and then kissed Vana on her forehead. Vana blushed and replied "I know." "So I suppose those cracks in its shell are to catch seeds" Samuel said "and as it grows up the plants in its shell grow with it" he added. "It's incredible that something can grow so much" Tamara said patting the turtles head.

"Hold on I have an idea" Vana said and she ran off towards the trees. The turtle had not moved much since it had settled on the beach, it seemed to be waiting for something though neither Samuel or Tamara had any idea as too what.

Vana returned a few minutes later hold what looked like pebbles, he placed several of them into the cracks and pits in the turtle's shell. The turtle began slapping its flippers against the sand, let out a large gasp and the started to turn around and head towards the water. "Those were seeds, weren't they?" Samuel said with a smile. "Well I doubted that it would find many seeds in the lake so I thought maybe the babies came onto land to get them"

Vana explained. "Why didn't I think of that?" Samuel asked. "Because I'm a genius remember" Vana replied.

The turtle returned to the water but this time it did not dive beneath it, it stayed on the surface that Samuel supposed was to make certain that the seeds it just acquired did not float away.

"Just think one day that animal will be a colossus" Tamara said. "Yep and if it's like every other turtle I know of it could live for over one hundred years" Samuel added.

Chapter 8

They had been in the mangroves for eight days and Tamara's patience was starting to wear thin. "I am really getting sick of this" Tamara moaned kicking up sand. Samuel let her vent for now as she threw stones into the water and discussed with Vana how they should handle this.

"The water was fun at first but even I'm starting to get annoyed" Vana explained as she sat down. Behind them they heard Tamara rip off a branch and started hitting the sand. Samuel nodded in agreement and rubbed his eyes. Samuel was unsure whether the mangroves were huge or if they had just been so delayed that it seemed bigger than it was.

Tamara was getting more enraged so Samuel decided he had to put an end to it, he walked over to her grabbed the stick, which Tamara tried to violently wrench from his grasp and Samuel explained and a gentle voice "Tamara you need to calm down." "Don't tell me to calm down!" she said once again tried to take back her stick so she could continue her attack on the swamp.

Samuel put his arm around her shoulder and said "Tamara you can't take revenge on sand and trees." "I can try" Tamara replied. He sighed and pushed Tamara down, they now sat side by side and Samuel asked "what's really the matter?" Tamara dropped the stick and rested her head, on Samuel's shoulder.

 She was quiet for several minutes and then she said "I wish we had turned back." Samuel smiled, stroked her head and kissed her scalp "yeah" he said sympathetically. "I'm starting to wish I had never left" Tamara added and then went silent.

After twenty minutes Tamara got up saying that the sooner they crossed this bloody place the faster they would get home. Samuel couldn't argue with that, he was happy that Tamara was cheerful again, so they crossed the next river and by the end of the day had covered more grounds than the previous two combined.

Then Vana spotted something on the horizon, they could see the lake curving and what was more there were no more trees just open grassland. "Just a couple more days at most and we'll be out of here" Vana said cheerfully. They went to bed with high spirits that night and for the first time in days were looking forward to tomorrow.

At midday, a problem occurred, up ahead they could make out the sound of people, there was a village here. "People actually live here?" Tamara said in disbelief. "What are we going to do?" Vana asked "I don't not want to just walk through the middle of their home, we'll get pots and pans thrown at us" Vana said remembering how most places had treated her. Samuel cleared his throat and looked her in the eye. "Oh, and Samuel will make things considerably worse" she added.

"Well I think our only option is to go around" Samuel said. "Is that really all we can do? We're running late as it is" Tamara asked disappointed. Samuel scratched his head and said "well you could probably go there and get along with everyone but you'd have to go alone."

Tamara thought about it and decided that it wasn't the worst idea in the world. "Look we can go around and when we set up camp I can go and introduce myself, hopefully they can tell us how far away from home and give us a few supplies" Tamara explained. "Are you sure they'll do that" Vana asked. "We'll they should at least be hospitable and maybe I can explain you and you can come on the next day" Tamara said.

Vana rubbed her hands and said "I'm not certain that's the best idea." Tamara gave Vana a hug and said "you need to have more confidence." Vana said she would see how Tamara's visit went and then she would decide.

They kept the village within earshot, making certain they would not see anyone when they were exposed. The last thing they needed was one of them paddling up the river and spotting Samuel.

They found an island, large with a circle of trees that kept they hidden from all sides. Vana built a smokeless fire in the centre while Tamara got ready to visit the village. "Are you sure that this a good idea?" Vana asked. Tamara looked at her as if she had said the sky was purple "of course it'll be fine."

They helped her towards the village, fortunately the islands were longer than they were wide so despite the tangle of roots it was far easier for Tamara.

When the village was in sight, they could tell it was far different from any they had seen before. The houses were built into the river so that at least half of building must be flooded, they were made from carefully bended wood, there was only one floor and it soon became clear why it was so different.

One of the villagers emerged from the water, he was around five foot nine inches tall, he had green hair and his skin was toned, ever so faintly, with the same colour, between his fingers were webbing that helped him catch the water as he swam. On his back was a leathery shell and he wore what could only be described as swimming trunks.

He flattened his hair but did nothing to dry it off and began to walk about the village which seemed remarkably empty. Samuel looked up at the sun, it was midday he supposed that aquatic people would probably find it uncomfortable. Right on cue the man looked up at the heavens and gave a look that could only be described as annoyance.

"Well here I go" Tamara said slapping her hands, on Samuel's and Vana's shoulders, and then walked into the open. Tamara paused for a moment to work up her courage and then called out "hello there."

The man was clearly confused as the voice did not match any he knew he turned around and saw the young woman standing in the sand. The confusion was replaced with surprise and then joy and he walked up to her held out his hand and said "Hello my dear, your new around these parts, what brings you here?"

Tamara smiled and shook his hands, it was cold to the touch, and replied "well it's a long story." "Oh, please tell it" the said cheerfully and the added "oh where are my manners I'm Aarav what is your name my dear?" Aarav's cheerfulness was infectious and Tamara found her mood improving by the second "I'm Tamara" she replied. "Well Tamara may I offer you a drink?" Aarav asked. "That's sounds lovely, so long as it's piping hot" he answered.

"She makes it look so easy" Vana said, slightly jealous. "Come on, we need to get out of here before anyone spots us" Samuel said tugging on her arm. They moved through the trees as quietly as they could but found no one, Vana believed that Tamara would be the centre of attention for a while and many people would make up any excuse not to leave.

Back at camp Samuel said "and what are we going to do for the rest of the day?" Vana had an idea she looked at Samuel and then gently pushed his shoulder. Samuel looked at where Vana had touched him and then looked at her, he then placed his hand on her shoulder and pushed her.

Vana pushed him even harder and Samuel did the same. Vana pushed him so hard that Samuel had to take a few steps back to stop himself from falling over. Before Samuel could retaliate Vana turned and ran. Samuel chased after her and shouted "come back here and take your comeuppance." "Never" Vana replied.

Back in the village a large crowd had gathered around Tamara, she was slightly unnerved by all the attention she was getting but it was far from unbearable. Once word had spread four village heads came out to greet her. Paloma was the representatives of the Kappa, the same people as Aarav though her hair was blue, she wore trunks just like Aarav but she also wore a bikini top.

The second was to say hello was Jabilo he could not leave the water so Tamara had to reach down over the river bank to shake his hand. He had sapphire blue hair and a long tail, with a ribbon of delicate skin flowing down his spine, were his legs would be, reminiscent of an eel, he too had webbed fingers. On his chest and stomach were ten slits, five on each side, that served as gills.

Jabilo explained that he was an Inkanyamba, Tamara though that he looked like the underwater equivalent of a Lamia. Jabilo felt that Tamara was a land living version of an Inkanyamba as he pointed this out and even suggested that they might want to switch lives for the day.

Next up was Shonagh, her skin was covered in a beautiful contrast of colours her stomach was pale, almost white while her back was leaf green. She eyes were bright red and her hair was a light purple. Her legs were astonishingly long but the rest of her body was so perfectly proportioned that it all looked natural and attractive. Her hands and feet were webbed but they also had these pads on the tips of her fingers and toes that Shonagh said helped her climb. Her race was called Agaly and if Tamara had to guess their traits came from frogs.

Last was Zali, just like Jabilo she could not leave the water, her hair was brunette and they perfectly matched her eyes. She had ten gills slits on her body similar to the Inkanyamba had no legs instead having a fish's tail, with a robust fin on the tip. Tamara needed no introduction was to what she was, Zali was clearly a mermaid.

Tamara told them about her trip around the lake and her companions. "Why aren't they here with you?" Shonagh asked. "Well… you see… Vana is a Dingonek" Tamara explained. This drew a large amount of murmurs from the crowd "are you sure that's wise my dear?" Jabilo asked.

Smiling back Tamara asked, with annoyance very clear in her voice, "why would that be a problem?" Jabilo knew very little about Tamara but it became immediately obvious that angering her would be a very bad move and he cautiously replied "well, there are a lot of stories about them and…" He was astonished at how difficult it was to continue his answer, Tamara's eyes were like daggers.

She sighed and asked him a question, the previous anger was gone, "how many Dingoneks have you met in your life?" "Well none" he answered honestly. Tamara smiled and said "precisely those stories you heard are just that, stories, if you ever come across one I think you will find that they are good honest people." Tamara paused and then added "I fact I would like to prove it to you all, if you will allow it I would like to bring Vana here tomorrow and you can all see for yourselves what kind of person she is."

The village heads talked amongst themselves and decided that the rules of hospitality override their concerns "very well we would all be very happy to meet her tomorrow and Samuel as well" Zali said with a cheerful smile. Tamara scratched the back of her head and explained "well Samuel cannot come, he is much too shy and I fear there would be some panic if he did come tomorrow." "Is he all right?" Paloma asked with genuine concern. Tamara waved her hand and said "oh he's fine he just doesn't do well when meeting new people."

"Well would you care for a tour of out village?" Shonagh asked. "I would love to" Tamara replied "though I can't go in the water it tires me out very quickly" she explained. "Oh, yes I've heard stories that Lamias get sluggish in the cold" said Zali.

To help Tamara out one of the villagers brought Tamara a raft that they used to transport objects that needed to be kept dry, such as fire wood, and two Merfolk pushed her along. "Sorry to trouble you like this" Tamara said as she sat down on the raft. "Oh, don't worry about it, I'm always happy to help and you've also given me a break from work so it's all good" the Merman replied with a smile.

They showed Tamara the meeting area, located in the centre of the village, which unlike at home was not a building but a pond cleared of all vegetation. The village head who had agreed to escort her while the other three carried on with the business of the day, Paloma swimming beside her, explained that a stone building was far too heavy for the soft sand and a wooden building that large would require too much maintenance.

They visited the market and despite being conducted on the river bank was very reminiscent of home, people chatted as they acquired various bits and bobs that they needed, from pottery to fruit. "Wait if you are water based how can you get apples and the like" Tamara asked as she passed a fruit vendor. "Well it's true the Inkanyamba and Merfolk can't leave the water, Agaly and Kappa's can, though not for very long" Paloma explained.

Their next stop was out into open water and Tamara was amazed by what she saw, along the shore line were vast fields of underwater crops. They were unlike any she had seen before but this was undoubtedly a farm. "What do you grow here?" Tamara asked in astonishment. "Well there's all sorts, water yams, lake grasses, and reeds, there are more but that might take all day" Paloma said.

She saw that there was a cut-off point in the fields and Tamara asked "why don't you plant more further out." Paloma said "if we did that then the Aspidochelone would gobble it all up." "The what?" Tamara asked. "You see them?" Paloma said pointing out at the lake. Tamara squinted and she could see that on the horizon were several island turtles and then it all clicked "oh so that's what they're called, Samuel will love this."

They ferried Tamara back down a separate stream and showed Tamara the residential district. Much like back home this part of the village was deserted during the day with only the elderly and the young chatting and playing in the water.

The younger children swam up to her, having never seen a Lamia before they were both nervous and amazed. A young Agaly girl asked her if she couldn't swim and Tamara explained that she could it was just the water was too cold for her. The girl looked at her and replied that river was very warm today and said that it must be hard being a Lamia.

Before long a whole parade of children were following Tamara around asking every single question that popped into their heads. Tamara was patient and answered every single question as best she could.

The trip paused for a moment on one of the islands, Tamara got of the raft and spread herself along the warm sand, the raft was convenient but she had been splashed more than once and she had started to cool down.

As she felt the heat returning to her body one of the elderly Kappa's approached her, she was small with greying hair and a warm face and she asked Tamara "would you like something to eat dear?" Tamara smiled back and said "I'm afraid that I only eat every five days or so and if I have anything to eat today I can give be stomach problems." Tamara then added "but if you could get me some hot water with some orange peel in it that would be lovely."

The woman returned home and a few minutes later she had a steaming cup clasped in her hand, which she had to hold above the water line to stop its contents from flowing down stream. She took a sip from it and immediately felt better. "So why are you out here my dear?" the woman asked "you don't seem particularly well suited to the water" she then added "I'm Elida by the way."

Tamara took another sip and said "well I just wanted to see what was beyond my village before my responsibilities meant that I would probably never leave again." "Ahh you've got some wander lust" The old woman said sitting beside her. "Yeah now I just want to go home" Tamara said.

"Say did you pass by a village on your way here? one in a scrub forest" Elida asked. "Yes, we did" Tamara replied. Elida smiled and said "I knew a girl from there, she was a centaur and we had a lot of fun, Rae she's called but I haven't been able to make the journey in years" the memory of her younger days made Elida laugh. "You didn't see her by any chance?" Elida asked.

Tamara was quiet and she tapped the cup as she tried to think about how to break the news to her. In the end, she decided that it was simply best to be blunt "I'm sorry but when we got there it was completely abandoned" Tamara explained. The group that surrounded Tamara went utterly quiet and Tamara kept looking at the ground until Elida, whose smile had vanished asked "What? Why? How?"

Tamara went on to explain what had happened to her own village just one year ago and that she believed that without Samuel and Vana to solve the problem the people had been forced to leave.

"I am sorry" Tamara repeated. "Oh no sweetie it wasn't your fault, at least I know they all got out of there alive, I'm sure Rae is settling in fine wherever she ended up, I just wish I could have seen her one more time" Elida said patting Tamara on her lap. "If you'll excuse me I want to be alone for a little bit" Elida added and slide back into the river.

As Tamara drank the last of her beverage she realised that Elida had forgotten her cup. Paloma realised this as well and said to a Inkanyamba girl "Bee could you be a dear and take this back to Mrs Elida." Bee smiled, grabbed the mug, and vanished beneath the water with a splash.

Back at camp Samuel and Vana had worn each other out, they sat down resting against the roots of separate trees. The pair of them were soaked from head to toe and sand blotched their clothes and hair. Both of them had forgotten why they had started their tussle but neither did they care.

"So, I win" Samuel said triumphantly. Vana spluttered and replied "you wish." They smiled at one another and Vana, feeling so relaxed, asked Samuel "Samuel what was your life like before you came here?" Samuel scratched his nose and said "I must have told you already." Vana shook her head and said "no, you always gloss over the subject." Samuel shrugged and said "it wasn't really that interesting." "I want to hear it anyway" Vana replied.

"Any part in particular?" asked Samuel. Vana ran her fingers through the sand and said "well what about that school and university you're always going on about." "Ok but I warned ya" Samuel said. "School was alright, I wasn't bullied or anything I left school with top marks in biology, then went on to do it at university, was on a foundation course for the first six month but then the lecturer saw that I was blowing all my peers out of the water so he had me bumped up to a masters" Samuel said with one breath.

He cleared up what he meant by masters and foundation degrees and then continued "was doing well, looked like I would easily finish the course top of my class, went home for the Christmas break and about four days before I was due to head back to Uni I ended up here."

Vana was quiet and Samuel said "told you it wasn't very interesting." Vana smiled, shook her head and said "No that's not it, it's the way you talk about it, you must have loved your previous life." Samuel nodded and said "yeah, it wasn't exciting or glamorous but it was quiet and it was mine."

Another pause and then Vana asked "Do you want to go back?" Samuel chuckled and said "Now that is a much more difficult question to answer." "Well give it a shot" Vana encouraged. "Had you asked me that question two years ago, I would have said, yes" then he added "if a magic portal had opened up in front of my cave I would have jumped through it without a second thought.

"But" Vana said. "But now I don't really know, I do want to see my mom and dad again, I want to finish my master's degree and get a job doing zoological research" Samuel said. Once again Samuel was quiet as he tried to put all his thought in to place after five minutes of silence he finally explained "but I don't want to say goodbye to Tamara, I mean she's virtually family by now, the thought of just leaving her behind is just terrible and I don't think I could just move on if I did find my way back."

After another pause, Samuel now was filled with a strange amount of courage said "and then there's you." Vana looked at him and said "what about me?" "I don't really know myself but the thought of never being able to see your gorgeous face again is worse than anything" Samuel said calmly "even if it is covered with mud."

Vana went bright red and looked at the ground and said "oh well, thank you, I guess." He looked away and said "sorry I didn't mean to make you feel uncomfortable." Vana looked back and almost shouted "Oh no it's nothing like that, it was very sweet of you and I appreciate it." The pair of them were quiet for what seemed like a decade until Samuel finally said "Do you want to go rustle up some grub." Vana looked back at him and said "that sounds lovely."

At the same time as Vana and Samuel left to find dinner Tamara was sitting beside the same river bank telling the children that were gathered around her about what she had seen on her journey. She mentioned the Moa, the Haast's Eagle, how Samuel had stupidly gathered one of its feather and what she had done to him after it was all over. They all laughed and Tamara felt a great rush, she wondered if this was how Aarush felt when he told stories.

The children started to leave after one parent after the other called them home for tea. "You're very good with children" Paloma said. "Well I'm used to dealing with larger groups of people" Tamara said. Then the gear started to turn in Paloma's head and she said "oh I see you're the daughter of a village head." Tamara smiled and nodded and Paloma added "yeah I can see why you would want to get away from it."

Paloma then said "you know I did something similar when I was about your age." "Oh, where did you go?" asked Tamara her curiosity now peeked. "I tried to swim across the lake and see what was on the opposite shore" Paloma replied giving a hand gesture to show how far it was." "Did you make it?" Asked Tamara. Paloma pattered her chest and said "yes I did." "What was it like?" Said Tamara. "Well the land was covered with a huge forest and growing around the trunks of each tree was a ring of flowers also…" Tamara then interrupted her and said "That's my home."

"How far away was it?" Tamara asked hoping to get a grasp on how much longer it would take. Paloma smiled and said "I was just like you when I finally reached the opposite shore, all I wanted to do was go home." Paloma cleared her throat and said "well it took me just over seven days to cross the lake so I would suppose it may take you around fifteen to get back home."

Tamara sighed and hunched over. "What's the matter?" Paloma asked. "Well I had said we would be gone thirty day at most, but at this rate we're going to arrive very late indeed" Tamara explained. Paloma pattered her shoulder and said "don't worry about it as long as you turn up at some point they're going to be ecstatic, trust me I know I told my parents I would be away for six days."

Now smiling Tamara said "Thank Mrs Paloma." "You're welcome my dear" Paloma replied. Tamara looked at the sun and said "I should be heading back to camp now or I won't have the energy to make it back." Oh, we'll help you, the two merfolk who had spent the time Tamara was on land chatting to their friends were called back and Tamara climbed back on to the raft.

Tamara explained where she was camped and her chauffeurs need no further instructions "you picked a good spot" Paloma said. As they passed through the river channels Tamara took the time to see how beautiful this place was, there was life everywhere, fish in the river, lilies growing on the water and the light streaming through the leaves made it seem like a dream.

The cluster of trees came into view and the merfolk deposited Tamara on the shore. Tamara thanked them and they left just leaving Tamara and Paloma. "So, your friends are behind those trees" Paloma said. "They should be, unless they went somewhere and didn't tell me" Tamara replied.

"Could I meet with them?" Paloma asked. Tamara blinked slowly and then replied "well I could call out Vana but for Samuel's sake it's best if you don't see him" Tamara replied. "I surprised anyone that nervous had the guts to leave his village" Paloma said with smile. Tamara smiled back though for a different reason.

Tamara walked to the entrance, Paloma following behind, and said "Vana?" "Yeah" Vana replied. "Could you come out here?" Tamara asked. "Why don't you come in here I'm busy" Vana retorted. "It's important" Tamara answered. "Fine" Vana agreed reluctantly.

Through the roots, they could make out flashed of crimson red and then Vana popped her head around a tree. Her annoyance turned to surprise and then Tamara saw no small amount of worry "you've brought a guest" Vana said looking at the ground and grasping hold of the tree trunk. Tamara smiled at her and explained "This is Paloma she wanted to meet you before you visited the village tomorrow." "If I visit" corrected her. "Now don't talk like that and stop hiding behind the tree you're not five" Tamara said.

Vana stepped out from behind her tree trunk, straightening her tunic as she did and went quiet. Tamara rolled her eyes and said "Mrs Paloma this is my good friend Vana, she's a little shy but a lot of fun once she warms up to you." Paloma spent a few seconds just looking at Vana, trying to see any of the stories she had heard as a young girl were in here but try as she might all she could see was a nervous young woman who just wanted to spend time with her friends.

Paloma laughed at how stupid she had been, walked to Vana and held out her hand "it's a pleasure to meet you Vana and I'm sorry if I made you nervous" she said with a broad smile on her lips. Vana looked at her and could tell from her expression she was honest, cautiously she took her hand and replied "that's ok."

"I looked forward to getting to know you better tomorrow" Paloma said cheerfully. The heat was starting to disappear and Tamara would soon need to sleep so Paloma left them in peace and told them to say hello to Samuel for her.

They waved her goodbye and entered the camp. Tamara was confused Samuel was up in a tree lashing logs to a tree "What are you doing?" she asked. "You tell her" Samuel replied. Vana explained "I don't like the look of those clouds" she gestured to some dark blotches on the horizon, "the colour of the sun" she pointed to it and finished "and I don't like the way the air feels it's too close."

"What does all that mean?" Tamara asked. Vana looked serious and said "a storm's coming, a big one." Vana then picked up a log from a pile they had collected after their dinner, "now you need to help us get this place ready" Vana said handing it to her.

It was a simple but sturdy set up, layers of branches covered by the tent tarp to keep the rain out and tied tightly to the tree trunks and staked deep into the ground. There had been no time to create separate accommodation so tonight they would all be sleeping together. "Are you serious?" Tamara asked. "Well you can sleep outside" Samuel replied "besides what's the problem we've slept together dozens of times?" he asked. "That was different, I was just a kid" Tamara said. Samuel smiled looked her dead in the eye and said "you still area kid."

Chapter 9

Once again Vana knew exactly what she was talking about. The rain, though it was more like someone had just turn on a tap over their heads, came down so suddenly that had the three of them had not already been inside the tent at the time they would have been soaked.

"That was close" Tamara said peering through a tiny gap in the tent's door. At the opposite end, Samuel was busy arranging all their things so that they had the most amount of room possible. Shortly after he was finished the wind picked up and began to blow the rain so hard it was virtually coming on sideways.

Then the thunder started to roar and through the double layer of tarp they could still make out the flashes of lightning. "I hate thunder storms" Vana said covering her ears after the last thunder clap. "Really I always liked them" Samuel said laying out the blankets. "Maybe so but I bet you always enjoyed them while you had a roof over your head" Vana replied. "Sorry" Samuel said. "Vana uncovered her ears and said "I'm not mad, just pointing something out."

The noise was becoming deafening and even Samuel was starting to wonder if he would be able to sleep tonight. Samuel wrapped one of his tunics around his face so that it covered his ears, "not perfect but better" Samuel whispered. "You look ridiculous" Tamara said with a giggle. "That may be so but I guarantee that within the next ten minutes you'll be doing the same" Samuel replied cockily.

In five minutes Tamara and Vana wrapped articles of clothing around their ears and Samuel said dramatically "the prophesy has been fulfilled." "What?!" Vana shouted.

Samuel decided that the sooner he was asleep the sooner this storm would be over so he lay down on his mattress. Even through the goose down he could still feel the logs and branches underneath, he fidgeted, tossed and turned hoping that he would find at least one position that was comfortable.

He never found out if he discovered a way that was pleasant enough because the next thing he knew it was morning.

"Must have been more exhausted than I realised" Samuel mumbled. As Samuel's brain registered the silence outside he realised that the storm was over, he did not move or open his eyes he just lay there appreciating the lack of noise, realising his ear protection was no longer necessary he removed it. It was funny he had fallen asleep very quickly but it still felt as if he had been forced to listen to TV static all night.

He wondered if he could catch another hour of shut eye but after a brief moment of relaxation he felt the branches underneath the mattress dig into his back. As his muscles started to ache he realised that he had to get up. He tried to but something was holding him down, he opened his eyes and saw that Vana was clinging to him.

Samuel did not know what to do, he was not bothered by this but he also felt it would be embarrassing for both of them if she realised what had happened, more so if Tamara found out. He decided to move her hands out of the way but found that Vana grip was like iron, no matter how hard he tried she refused to budge. The aches that had compelled his to get up now vanished. In the end, he just decided to enjoy the moment.

Vana stated to stir, half asleep her grasp on Samuel began even firmer, it was such a tight hold that it was starting to hurt. He tried to stop Vana from crushing his chest and at that moment she realised that Samuel was awake.

Her eyes snapped open and she stared directly into Samuel's eyes. "Good morning Vana" Samuel said. Vana only responded with blushing cheeks and he added "could you please let go before for you crack my ribs?"

There was a brief pause and then Vana let go and removed her hands with lightning speed. She tucked them underneath her blanket, turned away and then said into her sheets "sorry about that." The two were quiet and the only thing that broke the silence was the rustling they made underneath their sheets as they rubbed their hands together.

"Well I've managed to make you uncomfortable on two consecutive occasions, I really am a charmer aren't I" Samuel said. "Oh no, I was the one… who you know" Vana replied unable to finish her own sentence. More silence and then Samuel said "why did you… you know?" "After you fell asleep the lightning got worse and well I just wanted some comfort so I… hugged you" Vana explained. "Well it was very loud" Samuel said.

Samuel got out of bed and stuck his head out of their shelter. The cool morning air made his skin twitch and the sharp contrast of light stung his eyes. When his eyes started to adjust, he could see the damage the storm has wrought.

Floating in the morning tide were branches, twigs and leaves that had been ripped from their parent trees. Several of the support ropes that held the tarps in place had been torn out of the ground, the water was muddy with silt that had yet to settle on the bottom. A large branch was lying on top of their hut, the strength of the branches and the tautness of the tent sheet having stopped it from crashing on top of their heads.

"Did you hear a loud crash last night?" Samuel asked Vana as he brought his head back inside. "dozens of them, Why?" Vana replied. Samuel pointed above them and Vana looked outside. "That was close" Vana said. Samuel then reached over to her and pulled off the tunic she had used to block out the noise, "Thanks I totally forgot about that" Vana said.

The pair of them started to eat their breakfast, fruit again and Vana said "I can't wait to get out of this swamp" she was becoming sick of fruit. "It's good for you" Samuel replied jokingly chastising her "it keeps you nice and regular." Vana glowered at him and said "Samuel, I'm eating."

As they munched on his pomegranate Samuel felt relief as the awkwardness started to melt away, "why am I such a wuss" Samuel said inside his head. "I'm surprised that the storm didn't knock some trees down" Vana said. Grateful for the conversation Samuel replied "well I sure that somewhere at least one of them did."

"I hope the villagers are ok" Vana said. "Well you'll find out soon enough and you can lend a hand, that should shut up any of the holdouts" Samuel said smiling. "Will you two shut up, I'm trying to sleep" Tamara said into her pillow. Tamara then added "don't worry they'll be fine, those houses are well built" she paused for a second and then added "oh and Paloma says hi." "Wow it only took you twelve hours to tell me" Samuel replied. "I was sleepy, leave me alone" Tamara retorted.

The two of them did as Tamara requested, Samuel took a clean tunic and pair of trousers outside and got changed. It was tricky getting changed while balancing on tree roots, but Samuel managed it. The morning air was brisk but on the plus side he finally felt wide awake.

Vana joined him shortly after and they watched the water level drop and the river take back their usual shape. Fiddler crabs once again emerged from their hideaway but it became apparent that not everything had survived. As soon as they emerged they headed straight for the dens of their neighbours that had failed wake up and dragged their corpses from the earth and started to eat.

"Well aren't they lovely" Vana said. "You more than welcome to offer them a lecture on why cannibalism is wrong" Samuel said, taking a mental note to write about this later.

"Are you going to be all right today?" Samuel asked. "I'm nervous but I did it once before so I suppose I can do it again" Vana replied. "That's the spirit" Samuel said. "What about you? You'll be all alone for most of the day" Vana said the concern audible in her voice. Samuel smiled, it was nice to be cared about, and said "I'll be fine, I've got it all planned out, I can spend the morning wandering the mangroves, and then I can write about it in the afternoon."

"I really wish you'd genuinely moan and whine about something once in a while" Vana said "you're too noble, it's not natural." Samuel moved closer took hold of her hands, rubbing them gently and said, insincerely "I am so annoyed that you get to visit the village, I expect lots of presents when you get back and a back rub as well." "You really are a ponce" Vana said.

"So, you've finally asked her to marry you?" Tamara said. Both Samuel and Vana looked up at the shelter and saw Tamara's head sticking out the entrance. Both Samuel and Vana pulled their hands free from one another, Vana blushed and Samuel stammered as he tried to think of a retort. Tamara copied him and said "you two are just like Becanda and Hansad." "Thank heavens for that" Tamara said in her head and smile maliciously.

Tamara basked in the sun, as Samuel and Vana repaired the shelter Vana said "look we've got to do something." "You're right" Samuel whispered, "not today but when we are almost out of the mangroves we'll push her into the water." "What are to whispering about?" Tamara said looking at them "Nothing were just wondering about how much longer we'll be in this place" Samuel replied. Tamara then remembered what Paloma told her and then explained that they were roughly two weeks away from home.

She took a bit of flak for holding this information back for so long but Tamara explained that the storm pushed it to the back of her mind.

Tamara had warmed up and was ready to go to the village "ok let's do this" Vana said shaking her hands and they left Samuel behind. "He'll be alright?" Vana asked looking behind her. "Of course, he's Samuel" Tamara replied with a smile.

Outside the village both Tamara and Vana could tell that something was wrong, the sounds coming from its residents were not the usual idle chatter or mild annoyances that were the norm, they were cries of panic.

As Tamara led Vana to the meeting area, they found the village heads giving orders. Zali said to a large group of Mermaids and Inkanyamba "ok you lot search the western rivers." Shonagh and Paloma then explained, to the second grouping of Agaly and Kappa, "we need you to search the shore line but for heaven's sake do not get to far away from the shore, we don't want anyone drying out or cooking in their shells."

"What happened?" Tamara called out from the shore. The crowd turned to see the girls, there was some murmuring about Vana's appearance but Paloma was clearly relieved to see them both. She turned back to the crowd and said "what are you all waiting for, go, GO!"

The crowd dispersed and the village heads went to meet them. "Hello Tamara, you too Vana" Paloma greeted them and added "I glad to see you weathered the storm alright, is Samuel alright?" "He's fine" Tamara said "but what happened here?"

Paloma was clearly distressed and said "I'm sorry Vana but we will have to postpone the tour, a pair of children were out in the lake when the storm hit and they haven't returned." "What can we do?" Vana said instinctively. "I was hoping you would say that" Paloma said. The four of them explained that the waves generated by the storm were large, the village and everyone in it had escaped with minor damage but they could have easily pushed the children far inland.

"They are Inkanyamba, which means they can't move easily on land" Jabilo said seeing the confusion on Vana's face, he flicked his tail to show that Inkanyamba had no legs. "What are their names?" Tamara asked. "The eldest is a girl, she's sixteen and her name's Unice and she's with her brother, he's seven and called Cathal."

Zali suggested that they split up but Tamara remined them that she would not be able to cover much ground without Vana's help. Jabilo offered the use of a raft so that she could be quickly ferried between on island and the next. "What are you going to do?" Tamara asked. "We have to stay here and make sure nobody panic, though to be honest I would prefer to be out their" Paloma explained.

Tamara and Vana left, moving along the shore line, searching up and down each island they visited, they found a lot of evidence about the damage the storm had wrought but no sign of the kids. "I hope they'll be all right"

Vana said. Tamara patted her on the shoulder and said "they be ok, I'm sure of it."

Samuel had wasted no time after the girls had left. He had covered a dozen river channels and was currently doing the back stroke and, though he did not know it, was singing Strauss's Blue Danube.

He made landfall and jumped into the next river. He noticed a big lump moving slowly towards him, Samuel dived underneath the surface and saw the almost cylindrical creature, he recognised it at once, a manatee. Samuel was positively ecstatic, he moved to the mammal and touched its skin.

The manatee showed no fear and Samuel supposed that meant there were no predators in this river that could harm it. He noticed that it had no nails on its flippers with meant, if he was remembering it right, this was an Amazonian manatee. Samuel placed his hands on the animals face and said "ok look, you have to tell me how you got here all right, what are you doing in a freshwater mangrove swamp?" If he could talk the manatee ignored him and with surprising strength for such a slow-moving animal pulled its head free.

He inspected Samuel for several minutes, bumping into to him and gumming various part of his body. Though Samuel may very well have been fascinating he was not edible so the manatee swam away and started munching on the grasses that grew on the river bed.

Samuel, not burdened by the need to eat for seven hours a day spend a vast amount of time studying the creature's behaviours. He hoped that they would see another one before they left the mangroves, otherwise Tamara would have to draw it from description.

Using a herculean amount of willpower Samuel pulled himself away from the aquatic mammal and moved to the next river. He was having fun, without Vana and Tamara around he could spend as much time as he wanted looking, picking up or interacting with anything he chose.

Samuel's path brought him closer to the lake, he kept his eyes and ears pricked to make certain that he did not bump into any of the locals.

Samuel broke through the trees to find himself on a large sand island, almost completely devoid of plant life, apart from a barrier of brushes and shrubs that must have protected it from the storm. He saw two figures lying on the sand and he quickly hid behind the nearest tree.

His heart was thumping in his chest "that was close" Samuel said as he did not hear the screams that would have accompanied someone seeing him. He peered round the tree trunks, they had not moved. They looked like the Inkanyamba that Tamara had described, they did look just like an aquatic Lamia, their tails were mud brown, like Samuel's hair, though if his eyes served him right their hair was a gorgeous auburn. Then Samuel realised that something was wrong.

"Oh shit" Samuel said putting his hand to his mouth, he weighed up his options, it would be bad for anyone to see him but he couldn't just leave them like this. Samuel was not certain why he was doing this he already knew what he was going to do anyway. He stepped out from the tree and walked directly towards them.

Unice could feel the sun bearing down on her, her skin and scales were becoming bone dry, her gills burned at the lack of water and her fins were starting to crack in the heat. Cathal had not moved in some time and Unice was starting to worry that it was too late. She cursed herself for not heading home when she had the chance. She remembered the huge waves that had tossed her and her brother around like a rag doll. Through some miracle, they had managed to hold onto one another but it did not matter now they would suffocate soon, they were too far way for anyone to get here in time.

"Come on Cathal say something" Unice said giving him a nudge but he did not react and using the last of her moisture she cried. Through her exhausted sobs, she heard the sand shuffle in front of her. Using what remained of her strength she looked up, her mind was sluggish as the figure came closer but as her eyes adjusted and she was able to finally see what was coming towards Unice screamed.

Samuel winced as memories of his first meeting with Tamara came flooding back, but there was no time for pleasantries today. He ignored the girl, who was still well enough to move and headed to the young boy who had not budged an inch.

He checked for a pulse and the dryness of his gills, he was still alive but he would not be for much longer. "Get away from him!" Unice cried in mad panic but Samuel did not react this boy needed to get to the river and fast.

He picked him up and started carrying him away "put him down! Where are you taking him?" Unice said franticly but Samuel had no time for her. The boys skin was dry, his scales peeling in the sun and he had a nasty case of sunburn on his back, unfortunately Samuel could not run, the boy's weight and shape made it almost impossible. "Come back!" Unice screamed.

As fast as he could Samuel brought him to the water and dipped his entire body below the surface. He made certain that water was flowing around gills and for the first time he started to stir. Luckily, he was far too exhausted to open his eyes and kept mumbling "Unice what's happening?"

Samuel rubbed his head which made the boy smiled and he left him lying in the shallows, resting on a sand bank, that way the current would not carry him away. He returned to Unice who was staring at Samuel, the terror and horror in her eyes are palpable. He reminded himself that this was no time to be civil, she would never willingly except his help, so he put his arms under her and lifted her up.

She weighed more than Tamara did and grunted under the strain, to add to this there was a fine film around her body that made her slippery. Unice who had initially resisted was now paralyzed with fear. She stared directly into the monster's eyes, they were brown, his face hideous and her mind raced at what this thing was going to do to them.

Samuel looked directly into her hazel eyes. Then from a dusty corner of his mind he pulled something, something that seemed relevant at this moment. He wondered, as he took her to the river, if he should say anything at all but Samuel felt a need to say this.

So, with his feet crunching the sand underneath Samuel said

"Tis true my form is something odd,

But blaming me is blaming God;

Could I create myself anew

I would not fail in pleasing you."

His feet splashed in the water and as he lowered Unice in the cool liquid he added

"If I could reach from pole to pole

Or grasp the ocean with a span,

I would be measured by the soul;

The mind's the standard of the man."

Unice felt a fresh rush of energy as her gills absorbed the oxygen in the water. Unice stared at Samuel and said "you can talk?" Samuel smiled and replied, with a nod, "of course." She sat motionless until Samuel said "I think your young friend needs your attention far more than me."

She was snapped out of her trance and immediately dragged herself to her brother. He was a little worse for wear but he was breathing and he reacted to her voice. When she remembered that a human was still in the vicinity we looked around for him but Samuel was already heading for the trees.

Samuel looked behind himself to see that Unice was still there, a look of confusion on her face, he sighed and told her "go home Unice, your brother will need medical attention and your family will be worried about you."

Unice grabbed her brother and with one final look vanishing into the water. Samuel rubbed his eyes and said "I need a cleanser." Then he wondered if that manatee was still there and with a burst of activity jumped into the water.

Tamara and Vana had had no luck, they had met several of the villagers in their search but they had also seen nothing. At midday, they returned to the village hoping that someone else may have been more fortunate.

As they approached the village they could hear an uproar, Vana and Tamara understood that this was either really good or really bad. In the centre of town was a crowd of other people who had failed and come back for rest and a better plan. This was unnecessary because Unice and Cathal had returned. Her mother was crying tears of relief and joy that her babies were still alive.

Cathal was weak but the apothecary said that with some rest and a cream to ease the sunburn on his back he would be fine.

Her mom started to shout at Unice about staying out so late and through a storm no less. Unice explained what had happened, she then said that a human had saved their lives. The crowd went silent, Tamara and Vana looked at one another, the silence was broken by a tremendous laughter that emerged from the entire village.

Her mom told her to stop telling lies when Jabilo intervened and said that what most likely happened was she had become delirious in the heat and it was probably Tamara and Vana that had helped her, he gestured to the two of them.

This confused the girls as they had headed in the opposite direction to search for Unice and Cathal. The crowd turned to look at them and professions of thanks emerged from everyone any trepidation that people had had toward Vana was gone and the patted her on the shoulder and back. Their mother thanked them profusely and even Tamara was lost for words, for the time being they just went along with it.

As the crowd dispersed to find and inform the people who were still searching for them Tamara approached Unice and said "you say you saw a human?" Unice looked at her and replied "yes." "Can you describe them?" Vana said sitting down in the sand. Her eyes flicked back and forth between them and said "you believe me?" Tamara smiled and nodded and repeated "can you describe them?"

Unice rubbed her webbed fingers and repeated what she had told the group, though in greater detail "he looked exactly like the stories say" Unice explained. "What did he say exactly" Vana asked.

"Nothing at first he just picked up Cathal and carried him to the water" Unice explained "then he came to pick up me and while he carried me he told a poem." "A poem?" Tamara said in disbelief, she had never known Samuel to be anything near poetic. "That's what he did" Unice said with a shrug.

"What do you make of it?" Vana asked. "I don't know I mean he was human and he should have skinned me where I lay but he saved me and my brother but that can't be true" Unice said holding her head as though the idea was so impossible it would make her skull burst. "Maybe he truly wanted to help" Vana replied. She shook her head "Look I'm sorry, I've had a big day and I need to rest" Unice explained.

Tamara and Vana did not hold her up any longer and let her return home. Left alone on the sand bank Vana and Tamara discussed whether they should return to camp "we'll no one believes her so no one should go looking for him" Tamara reasoned. "And if we leave suddenly it might arouse suspicion" Vana added. They decided to continue where they had left of this morning and Tamara led her around the village.

They received heaps of praise and thanks from everyone they met, gifts were given in droves, in under twenty minutes they had received enough supplies to last weeks. Vana and Tamara excepted on Samuel's behalf, they would love to see the look on his face when they came back with all this.

Everyone wanted to know Vana's story with every clay jar and new top they piled on her. Vana had not experienced such an interest in her life for some time and it took her some time to readjust.

By day's end they had so much stuff that they needed help to ship it back, Unice's father kindly offered to push a second raft back up river as thanks for what he believed they had done.

He left them on the shore of their island and they waved him goodbye. "That was an interesting day" Tamara said. "Yep you can say that again" Vana said with a smile. When they entered the camp, they saw Samuel had started a fire and was scribbling on a piece of paper.

Samuel looked up as the sound of someone approaching hit his ears. "Did you have fun?" Samuel asked. "We could ask you the same thing" Tamara said dropping one of the sacks next to him. "What's that?" he asked pointing his quill towards the bag. "These are thankyous for what you did today" Vana explained dropping the second sack beside him. "You found out about that" Samuel said rummaging through the first sack. "Did you honestly think we wouldn't" Tamara replied. "Not really no" he said.

"I'm not sure this suits me" Samuel said pulling out a bikini top. "Oh you never know, maybe you can try it on tonight" Tamara said with a smile. "In your dream sweetie" he replied throwing it at her.

Vana sat down beside him and peered at his work "what did you find?" Samuel smiled and told her about the manatee "a pity you two weren't there he was a really friendly fellow" he explained. "You're a good person Samuel" Vana said with a smile. Tamara sat down on his opposite side and asked "so where did the poem come from?"

Samuel sniffed and said "I first read it when I looked up a man named Joseph Merrick, he was also known as the elephant man." "Why was he so famous?" Tamara asked. "Because he developed severe deformities in his early life, he was an outcast for most of his life but never forgot who he was or lost his self-respect" Samuel explained. "In his final years, he became quite the celebrity and he would end his letters with that poem" he added.

"How did he die?" Tamara asked. "I don't know for certain but I read that he wanted to sleep on his back" Samuel said. He then opened his hand wide around his head to help visualise what he was about to say next "his head was so large that they think it broke his neck when he lied down." "That's sad" Tamara said. Samuel nodded and said "yeah."

Chapter 10

As soon as Tamara was warm enough they set off, eager to make up for lost time, hopefully there would be no more delays. To help speed things up, the villagers had leant them a raft and told them about the fastest way through the mangroves.

They covered a large distance and rested on a sand bank, Samuel kept his eyes peeled for any sight of another manatee, he had had no luck so far but he kept his hopes up.

It was nice to eat a dinner that they did not have to personally scrounge up themselves. The greatest surprise were the water yams, Samuel had believed that they would be, well, watery but the tuber was packed with flavour.

Approximately one hour before sundown the mangroves stopped. Ahead of them was miles of open grassland, with small clusters of trees dotted about the vast expanse. Samuel fell on the grass and called out, rubbing the earth "look how smooth it is and it's so dry too."

The river they had followed had deposited them besides a rock formation and as they had promised the three of them left the raft they had used by it, to be collected later. Their packs were almost filled to bursting point "couldn't you have refused some of the stuff?" Samuel asked as he almost fell backwards. "I tried but they were so insistent" Vana replied.

Vana heard a splash and said "Samuel hide!" He darted behind one of the rocks and waited. A few moments later Unice, Cathal and their mother all popped their heads out of the water "Hello this is a surprise" Tamara said as she shook each of their hands. "We offered to go and collect the raft in the hopes that we might catch you before you left" Unice's mom explained "Oh I'm sorry I never properly introduced myself" she slapped herself on the head and added "I'm Habiba."

"Well Mrs Habiba I don't think we'll be going anywhere" Tamara said. "Why's that?" Habiba replied. Tamara smiled and explained "you gave us so much stuff that we can barely move." "We might have gone a little overboard yes" Habiba admitted. "What did you want to see us about?" Vana asked. Habiba smiled and said "I just wanted to say goodbye and wish you the best of luck."

Unice had not spoken since arriving her eyes were scanning the grasslands eventually she asked "where is Samuel?" "He's nearby he's just very shy and doesn't want be seen" Tamara answered "why?" Tamara asked. Unice looked at her and said "it's just Cathal said that he heard a man's voice not a woman so I thought that maybe it was Samuel that helped us."

Both Tamara and Vana were wary, there was clearly suspicion in her voice. Lies were easy to detect and both of them had to be cautious about how they answered, more so as they had already told her that they believed she had seen a human. "Well Samuel never said that he did" Vana explained, which was true Samuel had never blatantly said "I saved two kids today."

"Unice stop trying to make everyone believe that story, you were delirious from the heat, humans don't exist" Habiba said. "If Samuel really was the one who helped them tell him I said thank you" Habiba added completely oblivious to any possible connection.

"Well we're sorry to keep you, I'm sure you're anxious to go home but if you ever find yourselves in the neighbourhood we would love to see you again" Habiba said taking the raft away "Bye, bye" Cathal said waving. Unice lingered behind, squinted her eyes and said "I don't know what happened yesterday but if what I saw was true and if who I suspect really did save my brother I want to say… thank you." With that done Unice dived beneath the water and was gone.

Vana and Tamara went to Samuel who said, with true surprise "that was unexpected." He was right Samuel had saved people before but most thought that this was an accident or that his actions were part of some grand scheme to cause further harm. "I think she's like you" Samuel said to Tamara.

The girls nodded in agreement, there was one fundamental truth about most people in this world, almost everyone had a severe lack of imagination. Everyone blindly followed the lessons of the past and copied the technology and habits that already existed, advancement in mind or objects was rare. There were two glaring exceptions Samuel and Tamara, who always asked questions, it was this ability to imagine the impossible that had led Tamara to give Samuel a chance "it seems now there's three" Vana said.

Samuel then looked at Vana and said "oh you remember what we talked about?" Vana was confused for a few moments before the memory came back "oh yeah" Vana replied. Samuel and Vana walked up behind Tamara and Samuel said "lovely view" placing his hand on her shoulder. "Yep" Vana added. She winked at Samuel and in perfect sync they pushed her into the water.

Immediately they went into the river and pulled her out, smiling as they did. "You horrible bastards" she yelled as she clambered onto the grass. "Well you shouldn't tease people" Vana replied. They dried her off and helped her warm up.

"Well, we've still got some time before sunset, let's get going" Samuel said patting Tamara on damp head and the three of the set off in to the grassland. About two miles from the mangroves they set up camp for the night, they figured that this far away no one would spy Samuel by accident.

In this vast open space, Samuel kept an eye on Tamara though as far as he could tell she was handling it fine. As the new day grew on Samuel started to have mixed feelings about this new land. On the one hand, it was a relief to not have to weave and duck through rivers and trees, on the other it was a nightmare without any shade.

Fortunately, there was plenty of wildlife to keep him distracted, gazelles and blue wildebeest dotted the landscape, it was like a slice of Africa, though there was nowhere near as many as found on the Serengeti. "Maybe we'll find some giraffes or rhinos or elephants" Samuel said excitedly.

The next few days passed without any great surprises, Tamara caught up on most of her drawing and added more to her maps, she also concluded that both the grasslands and the scrub forest might be a good place to settle if he worse came to pass.

She had also made a very impressive drawing of a manatee despite never seeing one herself. Samuel wrote up more pages of his books and Vana busied herself collecting more flowers.

On day five Samuel thought he may have suffered some sort of concussion. In a patch of trees were the oddest-looking animals he had ever seen. They were over two and half meters tall with a head which resembled a horse, the walked on their knuckles like a gorilla, with long front legs and stubby hindquarters and ate like pandas. Their fur was brown with white stripes running perpendicular to their spines and at the end of their front feet were several long sharp claws.

"What the heck are those?" Tamara asked. "No idea" Vana replied. For all their strangeness, Samuel could have sworn that he had seen them or a picture of them somewhere and he could almost draw up the name.

"Calci… Cambi… Corri… Chalicotherium!" Samuel said. "What's a Chalicotherium?" Vana asked. "They are Chalicotherium" Samuel said pointing at the animals. "What do you know about them?" Vana said. "Not a lot they went extinct over three million years before I was born" he replied. Samuel put his head in his hands and said "this world makes no sense."

Samuel watched them use their long forearms to pull the branches down to their mouths "browsers" Samuel said jotting it down. Unlike any of the animals they had seen before the Chalicotherium were wary of the trio. As Samuel moved closer they stopped eating and watch him cautiously. "Do you think there's a village around here and the locals hunt them?" said Vana who was very familiar with this behaviour.

"That is possible but it could also mean that there are predators large enough to take them down" Samuel suggested remembering some of the monsters that lived three million years ago. The Chalicotherium went back to eating and even Samuel agreed that it was best to respect their personal space.

He spent roughly one hour making observations before Tamara insisted that they keep going "bye" Samuel said waving at the beasts.

Three days later Samuel and Tamara were sitting around a camp fire, Vana had left earlier to hunt for Tamara's dinner. Samuel had found a good piece of wood on the shore and was carving a model of the Island Turtles or Aspidochelone as the villagers had called them, he liked both names and used them interchangeably.

Tamara's stomach grumbled, she had put off dinner for a couple of days now, desperate to get home but finally Samuel and Vana had put their feet down and she would eat. Samuel grew tired of carving the trees on the shell and pick up another carving, one that resembled the Chalicotherium and worked on that.

A log on the fire cracked and Samuel was brought back to the here and now. "You ok?" Samuel asked. "Yes" Tamara replied rubbing her stomach "I just hope Vana come back soon." Another deep grumble and Samuel said "You really are hungry." She looked at him and said "that wasn't me."

Their ears pricked and they could hear something big approaching. Samuel grabbed his walking stick and rammed his knife into the top, while Tamara grabbed one of the branches from the fire.

They gathered around the campfire and kept a look out for whatever was coming. Then from behind Tamara's tent came another creature from the past. Almost two meters at the shoulder, four hooved legs and a broad, thick head filled with wicked teeth.

Samuel knew at once what it was, even older than Chalicotherium, "Daeodon" Samuel said, fear audible in his voice. "What?" Tamara said waving her touch as the animal. "Daeodon, it's a giant carnivorous pig" Samuel explained. "That's a pig?!" Tamara shouted. Even with this monster staring them in the face Samuel brain still reminded him "actually Daeodon was more closely related to hippos and whales than pigs." "Not now" Samuel whispered to himself.

The Daeodon roared at them, it looked starved, it had a wound on its back leg, this was bad it meant that it was desperate.

It took a few steps closer and Tamara waved her torch in its face while Samuel took a swing at it. The beast took a step back and roared again, it was a terrible guttural sound. The pair but the fire between it and them, it was clearly wary of the flames but hunger drove it on, it desperately needed an easy meal.

"Piss off!" Samuel shouted as the killer pig started to circle around the fire. The blade caught it on the face leaving a slight cut, the Daeodon skin was thick and leathery, it would take a truly forceful thrust to do any real damage. Still it had too many wounds already to risk anymore and took another step back.

Whatever was going on in its satsuma sized brain made it act reckless and shortly it was driven into a hunger fuelled rage, it wanted meat and it wanted it now. The Daeodon charged, it was hard to think that a creature that size could produce such a burst of speed.

It never reached its target because just as it crossed the half way mark Vana crashed into it knocking the beast onto its side, her claws penetrating its thick skin, spurting blood up Vana's forearms.

A Daeodon however is nothing if not tough and the animal quickly regained its footing, Vana's pupils were wide allowing the Daeodon's every moment to be processed. The beast sized her up whether it was that it had dealt with Dingoneks before or due to Vana's aggressiveness, the Daeodon did not register Vana as prey but a rival predator, as a threat.

The beast let out another roar to scare Vana off but she did not budge, she glowered at the animal and then charged. The Daeodon charged as well ramming into Vana and snapping its oversized jaws, it caught one of Vana's arms and clamped down hard.

Vana felt the pain but she had lived through worse and brought her other claw down hard, into the beast front leg. It stumbled and fell on top of Vana, who was winded by the animal's sheer bulk.

Through dumb luck the Daeodon landed on its feet and was keen to finish Vana off. As she watched it approach Vana knew that she need just a few seconds more to recover. Something flew over Vana's head and embedded itself in the animal's wounded shoulder, it howled in pain and Vana seized the opportunity, her tail lashed out and the stinger lodged deep into the animal's neck.

Vana's venom was a vicious cocktail of some of the most lethal neurotoxins in the world and the Daeodon was feeling the effects first hand. The beast swayed and shook its head the venom worked its way through its bloodstream, its organs began to shut down and the beast toppled over crushing Samuel's spear in the process. A few twitches and a half-hearted, almost tragic, whine later and the Daeodon was dead.

Samuel and Tamara quickly rushed to Vana's side, with Samuel immediately inspecting the damage to her arm. "Your walking stick got crushed" Vana said. Samuel utterly astonished by this show of selflessness immediately whacked her over the head. "What was that for?!" Vana shouted. Samuel let out a humourless laugh and said "you honestly think that care about a stick when you've been injured?"

Turning his attention back to the wound he noticed that the glossy chitin was covered in the beast's blood and had been cracked, a slow trickle of her own blood was oozing through the fractures. He cleaned the wound along with her face and took some medical supplies out of a bag and covered the cracks with a paste, a combination antiseptic and anaesthetic, he then wrapped the arm up in clean bandages.

"Your something else" Samuel said as he looked Vana over for any other injuries. "What?" Vana said. "That thing" Samuel said pointing to the Daeodon's corpse "a muscular, aggressive tank on hooves and you took it down… with your bare hands." Vana looked away and smiled.

"The antelope" Vana blurted out. "What?" Tamara said. "The antelope I caught for tea" Vana explained. Samuel rolled his eyes and said "I'll go get it." "No, I'll…" Vana said but Samuel cut her off, "you just fought that" once again pointing to the Daeodon "I think you deserve a break" with that said Samuel walked off into the grassland.

Tamara helped Vana up and led her into the camp though Tamara felt that she did not need any assistance "doesn't it hurt?" Tamara asked puzzled. "A little bit" Vana replied. "But it had teeth the size of knives how can it only hurt a little?" Tamara said. "I don't know it just does" was Vana's response.

"Thank you" Tamara said giving Vana a hug. "You'd have done the same" Vana said hugging her back. Samuel returned with the antelope slung over his shoulders, he reached for his knife and then remembered where he left it.

He went to the Daeodon and tried to flip it over but it was far too heavy. Vana walked over and with only a grunt she flipped the mountain of flesh. "You should be resting" Samuel said. "You would have been here all night" Vana replied. Samuel's job was not over though when the animal had collapsed it had buried the knife deep into its shoulder.

Sighing Samuel found the wound, rolled up his sleeve and forced his hand into it. He could feel the meat rip around his arm, strangely enough it was not exactly unpleasant, his knuckles brushed against what he though was bone, the knife had been buried deep. His fingers tickled the handle of his knife, he grasped it carefully, making certain his did not slice his fingers off, and with a firm tug pulled it from the beast.

He washed the knife in boiling water and asked Vana "does you're venom denature in heat?" "Does my what do what?" Vana replied. "Does your poison stop working when you boil it?" he clarified. "I've never been effected by it" Vana said. "You're a pillar of reassurance Vana" Samuel said. "I always love to help" Vana responded.

The following morning, before either Vana or Tamara was awake, Samuel took the time to examine the dead Daeodon, he also gathered up the splintered remnants of his walking stick.

He felt a pang of sympathy for the fallen creature as its lifeless eyes stared at him, Samuel closed its eyelid and patted it on its shoulder. He then pulled out three of its teeth, large powerful canines, and removed the gum and washed them in the lake. He found that the animal's teeth were well worn and had a lot of damage to them "you must have been an old boy" Samuel said.

Vana woke up and Samuel said "think fast" as he threw one of the teeth at her. Vana caught it easily and said "what did you get this for?" looking at the dead Daeodon. "So you can show everyone when we get back" Samuel replied. They rested as Tamara digested her tea, and on the next day they continued.

The grasslands stretched on ahead but in the distance, they could see thousands of trees. The land started to rise, the beach vanished and was replaced by a cliff. Their spirits lifted as the forest grew larger until they were just a few meters away, there was a gully in their way, with a river following through it.

For once fortune was on their side as a simple log bridge had been built connecting the two lands. "That explains why we've never seen on of those pigs before" Tamara said, the log was far too narrow for anything larger than a hare to cross unless of course they only had two legs.

Back under the cover of the trees, the all felt a huge rush of joy, even Samuel who usually complained about the overbearing heat could not help smiling as his nose twitched at the scent of honeysuckle and lavender. On top of this and especially after the Daeodon attack, Samuel started to appreciate how Tamara felt, he did indeed feel secure surrounded by the trees.

Before long however, as sweat started to gather on his brow, the old complaints came back. He left the cover of the trees to walk on the narrow strip of open land between the woods and the cliff face.

He peered over the cliff into the water below, even though they were several meters off the ground he could still see the bottom of the lake. Samuel noticed something, "Vana Tamara come look at this" he called. The girls looked down and Tamara said "what am I looking at?" "It's what you're not looking at" Samuel replied.

A few seconds later Tamara said "oh yeah" and then her brain clicked and she said "that's why." "Why what? What don't you see?" Vana asked. Tamara explained "there were no weeds or grasses on the lake bed." Vana looked again and said "yeah so?" "So, that means there's nothing for the Aspidochelone to eat over here" Tamara replied. At last Vana understood and said "which is why we've never seen them before."

Even though they were back in the forest this was a part they had never visited before, it was still unclear how long it would be before they reached home. As of today, they had been away from home for thirty-four days and the desire to see her mom and friends again was making Tamara literally bounce with joy.

In the distance, Samuel could make out a familiar sight, it was a cluster of highly eroded rock, reaching high into the sky, it was the old mountain, they were almost home.

Almost but the sun began to sink and Tamara began to slow down. They heard the roar of a waterfall and knew that they would be home by tomorrow, they set up camp besides the cliff face, there tents looking out over the lake. As Samuel settled down beneath his blanket he said "just one more day."

Epilogue

They were up and away the following day, the waterfall presented only a minor nuisance. The stream the cascaded over the cliffs was too fast flowing to swim but they had their solutions. Vana just jumped over it, putting Olympic long jumpers to shame while Tamara picked up Samuel and carried him up into the trees, along the branches and safely deposited him on the other side.

"I really need to build a bridge" Samuel said as his feet touched the ground. "I thought you were going to build a house" Tamara said as she clung to the tree trunk. "And a boat and tame a Haast's eagle" Vana added. "I'm still going to do all that, first it's the house, then the boat, then the eagle and finally the bridge" Samuel replied "or maybe it'll be the bridge then the eagle" he added.

In time the bird song and chatter of wildlife was replaced with the loud, indistinct drone of talking. Tamara sprinted towards the noise and the two of them followed. The trees gave way and there it was the village just as they had left it, "funny" thought Tamara "I don't remember it being this wonderful."

Samuel could go no further and they said their goodbyes "just don't leave me up there for weeks" Samuel said pointing to his home. "We'll try our best" Tamara replied. "Oh, and one word of advice don't run in there, just walk casually as if you just went out to pick blueberries" Samuel explained. Tamara and Samuel hugged and she said "all in all I think this was a good trip" and then she and Vana took the final steps home.

They entered through the residential area, and dropped their things off at home, the last thing they needed was to be barraged with questions while carrying these thing, Tamara believed that her back would snap in two. Vana took one satchel containing the drawings that Tamara had made along with a few trinkets they had collected.

No one had spotted them yet and that meant that they could choose where they went. Across the street, they could hear Caltha and Becanda hard at work and the girl's minds were made up.

They went around the back of Caltha's house and peered around the corner, Becanda was working but there was something different, Becanda was uneasy, as if her mind was elsewhere. Tamara knew why this was, they were five days late after all, so Tamara casually walked into the open and said "hello Becanda."

Becanda looked up and dropped her tools, the fence post she had been working on was tossed aside and Becanda barrelled into Tamara and knocked her to the floor. "You're ok!" Becanda cried and held her even tighter. "I missed you too" Tamara said, smiling and hugging her back.

"Everyone thought something terrible had happened to you, your mom has been worried sick" Becanda shouted, tears forming in her eyes. "What could go wrong? Vana was with me the whole time" Tamara replied. Becanda let go of Tamara and ran to Vana giving her the same treatment "don't ever leave again" Becanda said squeezing her.

Vana was taken aback by this treatment, she knew that people here liked her but she had not believed they had cared so much. Vana hugged her back a few tears forming in her eyes.

"Where is mom?" Tamara asked. "She'll be in town telling everyone not to worry" Caltha explained giving Tamara a hug. "Well we really should be going, we'll leave…" Tamara said but Caltha interrupted "nonsense we're going with you." "But what about your work?" Tamara asked. "Considering the circumstances, I don't think a one day delay will bother anyone" Caltha replied.

The moment that Tamara and Vana entered the busier parts of the village all work came to an end, word spread quickly and soon enough everyone knew that the girls were back.

Pancha was by far the most eager and she pushed herself to the head of the crowd, she thought about just what she was going to do to her daughter, she said thirty days not thirty-five. She reached the front and the moment she caught sight of Tamara any anger vanished, all that was left was relief that her daughter was home, alive and well.

She hugged her daughter and said "you're late!" "I'm sorry but we were slowed down by the swamp" Tamara explained. "Swamp?" Pancha asked. "We have quite the story" Tamara replied.

As the crowd listen with rapt attention Vana and Tamara described their adventure in excruciating detail. The Moa, the island turtle, the Haast's eagle, the abandoned village, the mangroves, the villagers, the storm, Samuel's heroics, the Chalicotherium and the Daeodon attack.

What almost everyone found impossible to believe was not the colossal turtle or the hell pig but that Samuel had saved someone's life. "Well that's what happened" Tamara said after she was asked "Really? I don't believe it" for the fiftieth time.

"Did you really fight that Daeodon?" one of the villagers asked. Vana held up her bandaged arm and said "yep." "Was it really as vicious as you say?" Vana put her hand in her pocket and threw one of the teeth Samuel had removed "you tell me."

The tooth was passed around and the younger children started to swarm the two of them asking to see more things they had collected. Vana took the opportunity to show off the flowers she had gathered, many of which did not grow in the forest and the boys and girls were clearly thrilled.

Tamara smiled and then showed the drawings she had made throughout the trip. The more fantastic animals naturally garnered the most attention but just as popular were the maps she had finished and the sketches she had made of the abandoned village, many villagers enjoyed seeing how they fitted into the surrounding world.

Handus walked up to Tamara as she was showing a white haired Cicindeli girl named Kyra where they had seen the Aspidochelone. "Well it seems that your crazy ideas are a big hit" Handus said sitting down. "In truth, they're not wholly my ideas" Tamara replied.

"You remember roughly a year ago, when we were standing in front of the sundial?" Handus asked. "Of course" Tamara replied "you said that I was just like Lamuel, always asking questions." Handus smiled and nodded "Well do you know where he got the idea from?" he asked. Tamara shook her head. "He noticed shadows moving around the support beam of a new house being built" Handus explained. Tamara was quiet and the meaning sunk in "you mean he would never have thought of it, if it wasn't for the hard work of others, you can't do everything alone" she said.

"That's right" Handus said. Tamara was quiet and then replied "but I already knew that, of course you can't make it all alone." "Then why don't you just suck it up and take the compliment?" Handus replied.

"Are you telling me that this whole speech was just to tell me to "take your compliment?" Tamara asked. Handus chuckled and said "pretty much." He then leaned over and whispered in her ear "tell Samuel he did good" he then got up and started talking to the crowd.

Tamara smiled to went back to showing everyone more of the world. Hansad and Becanda sat where Handus had been and Hansad asked her "so do you think that you'll be taking another trip anytime soon?" Tamara leaned back and said "you know what while I was out there I learned something." "And what was that?" Becanda asked. "That I really like sleeping in a big fluffy bed" Tamara replied.

For the first time in years Pancha followed Tamara up to bed and tucked her in. "I'm not a baby any more" Tamara reminded her. "You'll always be my baby" Pancha replied.

"That doesn't sound too bad actually" Tamara said after a brief moment of silence. Pancha kissed her on the forehead and said "sweet dreams." "Goodnight mom" Tamara replied.

As Pancha closed the door behind her, Tamara felt the comfort of her deep fluffy bed and looked around the room. She then smiled and went straight to sleep.

Outside a cave by the side of an old mountain, with a roaring fire providing the only light, the only know human in the world was sweeping up dirt and grim. No doubt everyone else was already in bed but Samuel was finishing the last of his clean-up. The cave had become filled with dust and the wicker fence had been blown down allowing animals to come in a pinch his vegetables. He had been forced to plant new crops in the limited time he had, as only three carrots had survived unscathed.

He had moved all his tools out of the dry room, mended the fence, repaired the tarp and after all that had been finished he had finally started sweeping the dust out of his home.

Despite all this he had still managed to get some leisure time in. On four separate pieces of paper were four entries the titles of which read Kappa (Homo Testudines), Inkanyamba (Homo Muraenidae), Agaly (Homo Anura) and finally Merfolk (Homo Dipnoi). Samuel had seen more of the mangrove villagers than they had realised. When he next saw her he would ask Tamara to do some drawings.

Samuel stretched his back, his muscles were killing him, and removed the slab, grabbing his writing he looked at the forest, he closed his eyes taking a deep breath and smiling, said to himself "I'm home."

Glossary

Chitin - A material that an insect's exoskeleton if made from.

Dingonek – A sabre-toothed Congolese cryptid with scaly skin and a scorpion's tail.

Lamia - A Greek woman cursed by the Gods, typically portrayed as a woman with a snake's tail for legs.

Greaves – Armour worn on a person's shins, similar to shin pads worn during sports.

Pupate – When a larva or grub transforms into a pupa.

Orion – A constellation visible from both the northern and southern hemisphere.

Aspidochelone – A mythical creature of tremendous size, usually depicted as a whale or turtle, that sailors would mistake for an island after which the Aspidochelone would dive killing them all.

Homo – the Genus that humans belong to, Latin for Man.

Inkanyamba – A legendary serpent that is supposed to live in a waterfall lake, usually beneath Howick falls, in South Africa the Zulu tribes believe it causes the seasonal storms.

Kappa – A mythical Japanese creature, with a beak and tortoise shell on its back, said to inhabit lakes and rivers.

Apothecary – A person who creates and dispenses medicine, otherwise known as a pharmacist or chemist.

Browser – An animal that eats the leaves of shrubs and trees.

Perpendicular – A line at a right angle to a plane.

Neurotoxin – Toxins that damaging to nerve tissue.

Denature – A process in which proteins lose their natural, complex structures and revert to simpler forms.

Printed in Great Britain
by Amazon